PILLAGED: A SCI-FI ALIEN WARRIOR ROMANCE

Raider Warlords of the Vandar #3

TANA STONE

Broadmoor Books

CHAPTER ONE

Rachael

I'd never intended to be a runaway bride.

Then again, I'd never expected that the imperial admiral my parents had arranged for me to marry would be such a decrepit old man. I shuddered as I thought about his bald head that constantly seemed to glisten with forehead sweat and his gaunt, wrinkled face.

"They can take their arranged marriage and shove it up their asses," I muttered, hurrying along the corridors of the Zagrath ship as the sirens screamed overhead.

Gathering handfuls of ivory organza in my hands, I tried to move faster—and ignore the straight pins pricking my palms. If only I hadn't been in the middle of a wedding dress fitting when the battle against the Vandar raiders had begun, it would make my escape attempt easier. The layers of gossamer fabric flowed from thin straps at my shoulders, draping across my chest and gathering at the snug waist, then belling out to the ground and sweeping into a train behind me. It was not an ideal outfit to be staging a covert escape in, but beggars couldn't be choosers, and at the moment, I was definitely a beggar.

I laughed darkly at the idea, but the sound was hollow to my ears. Considering that I'd been raised the only daughter of a rich merchant on the human settlement on Horl, I'd never known anything but comfort. I'd never left the planet before, or had any reason to do so. I'd been happy riding my horses, and going to the occasional dance where I would ignore most of my suitors.

Marriage was not something to which I'd given much thought, nor was the Zagrath empire that controlled our planet, but that was before my parents had decided to make a sweet deal with the empire. They got more money than they could imagine, and were elevated to the ruling class of Horl in exchange for me. Or, more specifically, in exchange for me marrying one of the imperial admirals.

"Fuckers," I said under my breath, flattening myself against the wall as a group of black-helmeted soldiers pounded by me with laser rifles held high.

But as angry as I wanted to be with my parents, I couldn't help but miss them and feeling a twinge of sympathy. I shouldn't blame them for the admiral being such a fossil. They'd only been told that he was the most powerful man in the Zagrath fleet, and that my children would be able to rise to the top of the empire. They'd thought they were doing what was best for me. At least, that was what they'd told me when I'd begged them not to let the Zagrath soldiers take me.

I hadn't even tried to reason with my father, whom I'd already heard talking about how he would spend his payout. But I'd clutched my mother's hands, hoping my appeal would soften her heart. Instead, she'd merely tugged her hands away, smoothed one of my glossy, black curls, and patted my cheek.

"I knew there had to be a reason you were so beautiful. This way, your beauty will not be wasted on the boys here." Her eyes glittered as she'd backed away. "You will be an imperial admiral's wife."

Bile rose up in my throat at the thought of screwing the old admiral. I'd been too startled by his age and his lack of hair to do anything but gape at him when I'd arrived on his ship and met him for the first time. For his part, he'd made no attempt to hide his tongue darting across his puckered lips and gaze roaming over my body as if he owned me, which, I guess he technically did.

"Well, not anymore you don't." I rounded a corner and fell in step behind a group of soldiers jogging down the corridor.

Despite my shock and horror, I had a clear memory of the layout of the cavernous ship from when I'd arrived and been escorted to my guest chamber, and if my guess was right, these soldiers were heading to the hangar bay. Luckily for me, they kept their heads facing forward, and their loud boots drowned out any sound my bare feet made as I hurried along behind them.

I wasn't completely sure what I would do once I reached the hangar bay. The Zagrath fleet was in the middle of a battle with at least one Vandar horde, and incoming weapons fire made the ship shudder every few seconds. The faint scent of smoke was another reminder that the ship was in chaos, which was precisely why I had to make my escape now. It was the only time a ship would be able to slip away without being noticed.

I didn't have long before the tailor who'd been altering my dress would realize that I wasn't coming back from the bathroom. I doubted anyone would pay much attention during the battle, but as soon as the dust settled, the admiral would know I was missing. It wouldn't take too much longer for them to determine I was no longer on the ship.

If I could get myself off, I reminded myself. One minor flaw with my escape plan was that I didn't know how to fly a spaceship. My first space flight had been the one which had brought me to the battleship. The only reason I didn't consider this a major problem was that I'd watched the shuttle pilot as he'd flown me, tracking his movements and noting which buttons he touched. I had a virtually flawless memory, which my mother had conditioned me not to talk about—"men want a beautiful girl, not a clever one, Rachael"—but which I was now counting on to get me out of this mess.

The soldiers I'd been following filed through a wide doorway, and I wanted to punch my fist into the air in satisfaction. I'd been right. We were in the hangar bay.

As the Zagrath fighters continued forward across the expansive space, I ducked behind a row of steel crates. Releasing the fabric balled in my fists, I caught my breath for a moment. Along with the sirens blaring overhead, the hangar bay vibrated with the hum of ships racing across the floor and out into space and soldiers bellowing orders to each other.

My heart raced as I peered out from my hiding spot. A female in layers of ivory fabric did not blend in with the steel-blue, imperial uniforms, and the gunmetal-gray ships surrounding me. There was nothing soft or frilly in this part of the Zagrath ship, and the moment I was spotted, heads would turn, and alarms would be raised. I needed to get to a ship as quickly and unobtrusively as possible.

I spotted a transport like the one I'd arrived on. It wasn't far from me, and no one was boarding it. Transports probably weren't in heavy demand during a battle, but it was perfect for my needs. Glancing desperately around, I didn't spot a thing I could drape over my puffy dress so I could get to the transport without being seen.

"Fuck me," I whispered, wishing I'd thought through my plan a little more before I'd made a run for it. If I got caught, I'd be locked up for sure, with no chance of escape before I was frogmarched down the aisle. A cold chill went through me, and I pressed my lips together. I'd just have to make sure I didn't get caught, because no way was I marrying that old fuck.

I scanned the space again, and this time I noticed that the crates I huddled behind were on a wheeled cart. If I moved slowly enough—which I would since the cart was so large—maybe no one would notice that the crates were moving themselves.

I bent low and grabbed the bottom of the cart, pushing forward as hard as I could. For a moment, nothing happened. Then the wheels mercifully started to turn. I pushed even harder, sweat trickling down my brow. Looking up, I assessed my progress. Only a few more metrons. I pushed as hard as I could, grateful that I'd opted out of sewing with my mother and had spent so much time riding. I couldn't make a cushion for crap, but I had the muscles to do *this*.

When the cart was almost flush with the transport, I gathered my dress up into as tight a ball around my waist as I could, and made a mad dash up the ramp. I threw myself into the pilot's chair and jammed my finger on the button that closed the ramp.

My pulse fluttered wildly as I braced for soldiers to rush toward the vessel and drag me off, but none did.

I didn't allow myself time to celebrate, though, my fingers working rapidly to fire up the engines. It wasn't hard to recall the pilot's movements, and soon the transport was moving across the hangar bay floor. I sunk low into the seat as I passed other ships and soldiers running to their vessels, hoping they were all too preoccupied to notice the female in the poufy white dress piloting a transport off the battleship.

When the path was clear, I accelerated across the floor and burst into space. The transition from the bright inside of the Zagrath hangar bay to the inky blackness of space was punctuated by red blasts of weapon fire, and it made me flinch. I banked my transport hard and flew underneath the belly of the battleship and away from the fighting.

The hard ball in my stomach relaxed once I'd put some distance between me and the imperial ships, and I realized none were following me. I'd done it. I'd actually escaped from the Zagrath.

"Yes!" I flopped back in my seat and let out a long breath, tears pricking my eyes. I didn't know where I was going, and for the moment, I didn't care. All I knew was I didn't have to marry that awful man or feel his wrinkled hands on me. For the first time in my life, I was free.

Then the ship jolted hard, and stopped moving.

CHAPTER TWO

Toraan

"You are sure?" I spun on my heel to face my *majak* as he stood at his console, his dark hair falling forward while he studied the readouts.

He gave a single nod and looked up to meet my eyes. "Positive, Raas. There is only a humanoid female on board the Zagrath shuttle."

I pivoted to stare out the wide glass that stretched across the far end of the command deck. The dull gray of the enemy shuttle was easy to track across the blackness of space, and the ship was not going fast. It hadn't accelerated much since leaving the enemy battleship, almost as if it were slinking away and trying not to attract attention.

"And not a Zagrath?" I asked.

"The Zagrath are humanoid, but this female is not one of them."

My fingers buzzed as I drummed them across the iron hilt of my battle axe. Why would a Zagrath transport leave during a battle against two Vandar hordes, and why would it only contain one female? As far as I knew, the empire did not employ female soldiers or pilots, and never anyone who wasn't a pure-blood Zagrath.

I narrowed my gaze at the small ship, so ill-suited for battle. The female inside was clearly escaping, and using the heat of the battle to slip out undetected. It was a clever strategy, and one that would have worked if my horde had not been hovering unseen just outside the battle.

In the corner of the view screen, bursts of red laser fire lit up the sky, as the battle between my two brothers' hordes and the Zagrath fleet raged on. I'd determined that the Vandar had the advantage and would soon defeat the enemy, so had chosen not to drop our invisibility shielding. It had been too long since I'd laid eyes on either of my older brothers, and a battle was not the time for a family reunion. At least, not for me.

I could barely remember my brothers. I'd been a child in arms when they'd left—first Kratos to apprentice under our father and then Kaalek to serve a distant Raas in a far-away sector. Neither had returned before I'd joined our uncle as a raider apprentice, and I suspected they would not even recognize the warrior I'd become. Although we shared dark hair, I'd been told I was the only one who'd inherited our mother's hazel eyes. I pushed thoughts of my mother and brothers aside, and focused on the hunt at hand.

"Continue to follow until we are well away from the enemy battleship," I ordered, my pulse quickening. "Then lock on, and bring the transport in to our hangar bay."

My *majak* cocked an eyebrow almost imperceptibly. "We are bringing a female on board?"

It was no secret among the hordes that my eldest brother, Raas Kratos, had taken a human female as his captive and then made her his Raisa. The news had spread throughout the Vandar hordes as if our ships were networked, instead of spread throughout the galaxy. And then the second oldest of my brothers, Raas Kaalek, had taken the human's sister as punishment for her setting the empire on Kratos. So, human females were no longer the mystery to Vandar hordes that they had been, although it could not be said they were commonplace, either.

"Yes, Rolan." I met his gaze and saw curiosity, not challenge. "I want to know why the empire had a human female on their ship, and why she took the risk of escaping during a battle."

A knowing look crossed my *majak's* face. "You see a possibility for a strategic advantage."

Rolan knew me too well. He had also served under my uncle, Raas Maassen, who had trained both of us in the importance of long-term strategy. Instead of thinking in single battles and victories, we'd been taught to think many moves ahead of our opponents, and play the long game. It was why I'd inherited the largest horde of ships of any Vandar Raas, and why my ships were more technologically advanced than any others.

"Perhaps I only wish to offer aid," I said.

Rolan stifled a laugh. "Yes, Raas. And what about the Zagrath battleship?"

I waved a hand in dismissal. "Leave it. We do not need the spoils." What I didn't say was that I much preferred the pursuit of the small ship and the fleeing female. It fired my blood to give chase without being seen.

The female in the enemy transport had no idea a horde of Vandar raiders were stealthily shadowing her, even as she might be congratulating herself for escaping from the empire. I imagined the creature flying unawares, checking her sensors and her view screen and seeing no indication that we were there. The predator in me savored the chase, my heart pounding as we closed in on the vessel and the unsuspecting female.

My battle chief emerged from his *oblek* on one side of the command deck. Although he had no prisoners to interrogate, he often worked on battle strategy in the dark chamber where weapons hung from chains on the walls.

"Viken." I inclined my head to the door leading off the command deck. "Join me in welcoming our prisoner?" I then looked at Rolan. "You have the command deck while I am gone."

My *majak* clicked his heels and turned sharply back to his console.

My battle chief's pupils flared with interest as he walked over to join me. "A prisoner? An enemy fighter?"

I took long strides to meet him. "A human female running from the enemy."

Confusion flashed across his face, followed by disappointment. There would be no interrogation for him and no enemy secrets to procure. "We are taking a female on board?"

I shrugged as we left the bridge, winding our way down the dark labyrinth of iron stairs and suspended walkways that made up the interior of a Vandar ship. My uncle had once described it like a spider's web with the ability to shift and change, unlike most ships with enclosed corridors and the inner-workings hidden behind walls. It certainly made it harder for our enemies to board our ships, as most fighters who'd never been on a Vandar ship were overwhelmed and easily lost in the maze.

I leapt the last two steps of a winding staircase, my boots echoing as they hit the hard steel walkway, and waited for Viken to land next to me. "I need to know why a female is running from our enemy."

Viken made an approving noise. "Our enemy's enemy is our friend."

"Something like that."

"We do not usually take prisoners, Raas. If she is not meant for my *oblek*, where shall we put her?"

Even though it was my habit to think several moves ahead, in this case, I had not. I only knew we had to stalk the transport and capture it. I'd even thought so far as to imagine the questions I would ask, but it had not occurred to me that she would be staying.

"If she can provide us with no information about our enemy, there will be no reason to keep her. The Vandar have no war with the humans."

"Only the ones who collaborate with the empire."

Anger made my face heat, as I thought about those who enabled the empire to keep their stranglehold over the galaxy. We had blown enough of those traitors out of the sky. "Only those."

Viken paused when we reached the doors to the hangar bay. "And if she is a spy for the empire?"

I stopped short. This had also not occurred to me. I, who had been so carefully trained in strategy and out-thinking my enemy and even my fellow Vandar, was so excited by the chase that I was not assessing the situation with the cold detachment it needed.

"You are right, Viken." I put a hand on my battle chief's shoulder. "This might not be what it seems. This could be a clever Zagrath plot."

"They do not happen often, Raas, but they do happen."

I allowed myself a grin. Viken did not think much of his imperial counterparts, but he knew to be suspicious. The Zagrath could never be trusted.

"We will proceed with caution." I led the way into the expansive hangar bay, with rows of sleek, black vessels waiting to be boarded. Their curved wings extended like claws and their noses pointed toward the opening into space—only a wall of pulsing energy keeping everything from being sucked out of the gaping mouth at the far end.

Viken joined me in standing in the center of the space as our tractor beam pulled the enemy transport through the energy field and deposited it in front of us. When the beam disengaged, the ship sat completely motionless. The ramp did not lower, and no sound came from inside.

I exchanged a look with Viken before he took a long step to the ship and pounded a hand on the hull. Another long moment and the ramp started to lower, the metal hitting the floor with a resounding thud. Even though I doubted the female would be armed, I rested my hand on my axe and saw my battle chief do the same.

"*Vaes!*" I called out. "You are now in the domain of the Vandar. Show yourself."

When she emerged and stood at the top of the ramp, I stopped breathing.

CHAPTER THREE

Rachael

I'd had plenty of time to panic while my ship had been immobilized and then pulled toward something I couldn't see. I wasn't great with the readouts on the transport, but the sensors didn't show anything out there. Not that the readouts mattered to whatever had me in their tractor beam. Trying to regain control hadn't worked, either. I'd punched every button I could, jamming my fingers on the console until I wanted to scream. I'd finally slumped over in the pilot's chair, my arms on the console as a few lights blinked impotently.

"Vandar," I whispered to myself, as if saying the name any louder would summon the terrifying raiders. "It has to be them."

I peered out the front of the ship and rubbed my arms. My stomach tightened just thinking about the bloodthirsty creatures who flew in hordes of invisible ships, raiding ships and planets with equal fervor. They'd never attacked Horl, but only because the empire had such a strong defense system. Not even the Vandar could slip through the blockade that flew above our planet.

But they'd had no problem tracking me. I could have kicked myself. I'd been so focused on getting away from the admiral that I'd forgotten that I wouldn't need to escape only the Zagrath. Since the empire was battling the Vandar, I needed to avoid them, as well.

"So much for that brilliant plan."

I stood and paced a small circle in the compact ship, thinking over my options. They'd clearly tracked me from the imperial battleship. Either they wanted me as a pawn to use in exchange with the empire—did the Vandar do bargaining?—or they intended to punish me for being in a Zagrath ship. I thought for a moment about which would be worse, but the answer was quickly clear.

I'd rather be tortured than sent back to the admiral. I'd just tell the Vandar that I requested asylum, and hope they would show me mercy.

I stumbled forward and braced myself against the back of the pilot's chair as my ship passed through some sort of energy field. Suddenly, I was inside the hangar bay of a ship. A large ship. Rows of glossy, black vessels stretched out in all directions, and steel beams crisscrossed high overhead, the metal glinting through the low lighting.

My mouth went dry as the tractor beam set my ship down, and I spotted two figures standing with their feet wide. Shit. Was this what raiders looked like? Suddenly, my plan to ask for asylum didn't seem so great.

For one thing, the two males were larger than anyone I'd ever seen before. The Zagrath were taller than other humans—a result of centuries of the best resources and care—but these aliens were massive. Not only would they easily tower over a Zagrath, they appeared to be made entirely of muscle, with broad chests covered with black swirling lines and huge, bulging arms. It was easy to see all those things, because they only wore leather skirts held up by wide belts.

At least one of them did. The other also wore brown straps crisscrossing his chest, presumably to hold his shoulder armor in place. One of his arms was covered in metallic, scaled armor, and the other capped with stiff leather. Both of the Vandar had long, dark hair, and round-bladed weapons hanging from their waists—and… tails.

I gripped the back of the chair harder to keep myself upright. Long tails with furry tips swished behind them, making them seem like predators preparing to strike.

Don't be absurd, I told myself. *The Vandar don't eat people. Do they?*

I glanced down at the ridiculous layers of ivory organza I wore. How was I supposed to negotiate with these imposing males when they looked like *that* and I looked like *this*?

There was a loud thumping on the outside of my ship, causing me to jump and put a hand over my heart. Then one of them bellowed something—a Vandar word I couldn't understand and then an order I could.

"It's all right, Rachael," I told myself. "Everything is going to be all right. You didn't do anything wrong. At least, not to them. The Vandar aren't your enemy."

I took a deep breath to calm myself then pressed the button to lower the ramp. I waited until it hit the floor and clenched my hands into tight fists. I had to look tough or these warriors wouldn't respect me.

"You're a badass, Rachael," I reminded myself in a whisper as I walked to the top of the ramp. "You stole a ship and escaped from the empire. If you can do that, you can handle this."

I paused for a moment, looking from one Vandar to the other. Neither of them spoke, so I walked down the ramp as regally as I could manage, considering my entire body was shaking.

"My name is Rachael," I said, hating the quaver in my voice but talking louder to hide it. "I'm a citizen of Horl. I have escaped from the Zagrath ship and request asylum from the Vandar."

"Asylum?" The warrior without the extra armor asked, his expression stunned as he glanced at the other Vandar.

I nodded, but focused my response on the warrior with the extra armor. He was clearly the one in charge. "Will you grant me asylum?"

The warrior blinked a few times and cleared his throat. "You know we are Vandar?"

"Aren't you?"

"Raas," the other warrior said, as if he couldn't help himself. "You are addressing Raas Toraan of the Vandar."

I wasn't sure if I was supposed to bow or curtsy or what, so I did a combination of the two. "Sorry. Raas Toraan."

When I looked up again, I could have sworn I saw the Raas' lips quiver, but his eyes stayed locked on mine.

"The Vandar do not provide asylum," he said. "We are raiders."

"I know." My resolve was slipping, and panic was clawing its way up my throat. "But I can't go back to him."

"Him?"

"Admiral Kurmog of the Zagrath fleet. I'm supposed to marry him."

Now the Raas' dark eyebrow twitched. "You are a Zagrath bride?"

I clenched my fists harder, and the fingernails bit into my flesh. "Not by choice. My parents agreed to an arranged marriage, but I can't do it. I won't."

"You are not his one true mate?"

I narrowed my eyes at him. "One true mate? Hardly. I just met him, and he's a creepy old man."

"So, you wish the Vandar to give you asylum from this man and hide you?"

I let out a small breath of relief. Now he was getting it. "Yes. Thank you."

"Until when?"

"What?"

"If you do not wish to be returned to the Zagrath, and you most likely cannot return home, how long do you expect the Vandar to keep you hidden?" He shifted on his feet. "Or do you intend to live on our horde ship for the rest of your life? The Vandar do not have females on our ships, nor do we have guest quarters."

I hadn't thought that far. What did I expect these brutal raiders to do with me? I swallowed hard as I thought of all the things that could happen to me on a ship filled with violent males. "I...I don't know. I just hoped you might help— "

"The Vandar liberate the galaxy from imperial rule," he said, cutting me off. "We do not provide sanctuary for unhappy females. But I also cannot let you return to the skies." His eyes cut to my dress. "You will not last long on your own."

He was going to return me to the Zagrath. No, no, no, no, no. I couldn't do it. I couldn't spend my life with that disgusting old man.

My heart hammered wildly in my chest, and I grasped the Raas' arm. "Please don't turn me over to the admiral. If you keep me, I'll tell you everything I know about his plot against the Vandar."

CHAPTER FOUR

Toraan

I had no intention of turning her over to the Zagrath. I told myself I would never do such a thing because the Vandar did not aid the empire in any way, but the truth was I couldn't stand the thought of her with the admiral, either.

The moment she'd appeared at the top of the ship's ramp, I'd lost my ability to think. Rachael was unlike any female I'd ever seen before, and my heart hammered in my chest like I was going into battle and not standing on the hangar bay of my own warbird. It was easy to understand why the Zagrath admiral coveted her, and why her parents had been able to arrange a union with the most powerful man in the imperial military. By any measures, she was breathtaking.

She was smaller than me, but any human would be, with curves that were accentuated by the drape of the white fabric over her warm, brown skin. Black, glossy curls fell around her bare shoulders, but what drew me to her like a *carvoth* to a flame were her amber eyes that flashed with intensity. The human might be at my mercy, but she was no victim.

My mind went back to my first love and the flash of intensity in Lila's gaze when she'd looked at me. She'd also had a fiery spirit that had drawn me to her—a fire that had ended up leaving nothing but scorched wreckage where my heart had been. Remnants of rage roiled in my belly, and I forced it down along with the bad memories, reminding myself that females had caused me little but pain. This one might be beautiful, but that did not mean she wasn't a threat.

"Raas?" Viken's voice was low but questioning.

I gave my head a brusque shake, pulling my eyes back from where they'd wandered to her plump lips. "Did you say the admiral has a plot against the Vandar?"

She nodded, tugging her bottom lip up with her teeth.

"Aside from their usual plan to battle us when we fight their incursions?" Viken asked when I was again silent.

"There's more than that," she said. "And I'll tell you everything I know if you give me asylum."

I held her gaze, searching for deception. I saw none, but I'd been deceived before.

"Why should we believe that you know imperial battle strategy?" I snapped, even though I'd already decided to let her stay. I wanted to know more about her situation on the enemy ship, but I did not want her to think she'd succeeded in pleading her case. For a reason I couldn't explain, I needed to know if the admiral had claimed her, although the thought made me want to slit the Zagrath's throat. "Did the admiral engage in pillow talk?"

She reared back as if I'd struck her. "I did not share a bed with him." She wrinkled her nose. "I refused to share quarters with him until after the ceremony."

That fact pleased me more than it should have. I did not know this female, and the goings-on of the empire—the brides they took or the matches they arranged—should not concern me. But it did. I admired the female for refusing the admiral in as many ways as she could, even as I cautioned myself to harden my heart.

"Then he included you in strategy meetings?" I asked.

She folded her arms across her chest, her cleavage popping above the draped neckline of her dress. "No. If you must know, he ignored me. That's why I know so much."

I cocked my head and waited for her to continue as my own heartbeat steadied.

"He thought I was a brainless female, so he didn't watch what he said in front of me. He also didn't know how to talk to women, or didn't want to bother, so he invited officers to every meal we shared. Since he didn't care about making conversation with me, he talked to them about their missions and plans."

When she stopped speaking, she locked eyes with me, as if challenging me to dare make the same mistake as the admiral.

"He sounds like a fool."

One corner of her mouth twitched. "He was. I hope the Raas is not one, as well."

Beside me, Viken sucked in air. No one spoke to a Raas like that. Not and lived to talk about it.

I did not mind her speaking freely, although I could not have her openly challenging me. I took a long step, closing the distance between us and towering over her. She tried to back up, but I whipped my tail around her legs to keep her from moving. I lowered my head until my lips were so close to the shell of her ear I could have nipped it. "You will find I am nothing like a Zagrath, little human. But you should never mistake my temperance for weakness. I will allow you to stay on my warbird, but only because your information will aid my strategy. I do not tolerate deceit. If I discover that you have been dishonest with me or that you are working for the empire, I will not hesitate to marry you off to the old admiral myself."

Her breathing was shallow, the puffs of air warm on my neck. I ran my tail underneath the fabric of her dress until I found the soft skin of her leg, dragging my furry tip from her ankle to her inner thigh. The pulse on the side of her throat throbbed, but she nodded. "I understand, Raas. I am not lying."

"Good." I unwound my tail, letting the sensitive tip linger on her velvety skin a moment longer before pulling it away. "As long as we understand each other."

I stepped back to stand shoulder to shoulder with my battle chief, struggling to control my own breath. Touching her had sent frissons of pleasure through my body, and my tail trembled from the contact. Even my fingers tingled, and they'd come nowhere close to the female.

It was her beauty, I told myself. I was enraptured by her—and starved for female touch. It had been a long time since my horde had stopped at a pleasure planet, or arranged to dock with a pleasure ship. Pleasurers were a weak substitute for genuine female companionship, but I'd given up any hope of that long ago.

Many Vandar raiders anticipated the time when they would leave the horde in space and take a mate on one of our secret colonies. For me, that was not an option. The Vandar female I'd been convinced would be my one true mate had taken another male, breaking my heart and turning it to stone. After her rejection, I'd sworn off the idea of a mate altogether. I was resigned to living my life in space as a Raas, enjoying the occasional pleasurer, but never allowing myself to feel anything for them. Not that it was difficult. Pleasurers were skilled and practiced and unemotional, and made no secret of it.

I eyed Rachael thoughtfully. This female was not trained to pleasure and serve. There was a spark in her eyes. She'd stolen a ship and escaped from a marriage she did not want. She would not submit to just anyone. The thought of her rebellion and fire made my pulse race. She was just the challenge I needed.

I pivoted to Viken. "Take her to the chamber attached to my quarters."

His pupils widened even as he kept his face solemn. "The Raisa chamber?"

I flinched at that word. My uncle had designed his warbird with a sleeping chamber for his mate to travel with him. Although it was not Vandar tradition, he had never been one to follow rules slavishly—one of the many reasons he had not seen eye to eye with my own father. But his Raisa had died of a rare illness before she joined the ship. He'd never taken another mate and never used the Raisa chamber. But still, it was attached to the Raas quarters I'd inherited, and now it would be put to use, even if the name did not fit.

"Yes, Viken." I flicked my gaze to him and then away quickly. "I prefer to question her there instead of your *oblek*. I believe it will be more productive."

My battle chief's brow quirked slightly, before his face resumed its stern expression. He stepped forward, taking her by the arm and leading her away.

As she passed me, I curled my tail around her forearm to stop her. I bent low, breathing in the sweet scent of her. "I will come to you soon. You should be prepared."

She swallowed hard, her eyelashes fluttering. "Prepared?"

"You have come onto a Vandar warbird to ask us to protect you from the empire and keep you hidden from your fiancé, who is an imperial admiral. We will do this at risk to our horde, but only if you are prepared to give us—me—something of value."

"I told you I have information."

I let my gaze drift to her lips, which she licked nervously. "Yes, information. Let us hope it is as valuable as you claim, or you should consider what else you are willing to give me."

She lifted her chin. "You will not be disappointed, Raas."

I stepped back, releasing her arm from my tail's grip, and watched Viken lead her away. I growled and jerked my head away from the sight of her.

This is all a part of your strategy, I reminded myself. *Nothing more. She is nothing more than another pawn in the game.*

My stomach twisted. A beautiful, dangerous pawn who could be my undoing.

CHAPTER FIVE

Rachael

I pushed myself up in bed and swung my feet over until they hit the shiny, black floor. How long had I been sleeping? I'd lost all track of time. It even took me a moment to remember where I was, and what had happened. It had been disorienting enough to be led through the strange, dark raider ship with its seemingly endless series of staircases and bridges suspended on top of each other, but the room I'd been led to was even more unfamiliar.

At the time, I'd barely had long to take it all in before I'd collapsed on the bed in exhaustion, the stress of the escape and capture washing over me. But now I was awake, and trying to absorb how different my new surroundings were from everything I'd ever known.

My house on Horl had high ceilings, and bright windows that overlooked rolling pasture. Tall trees had stretched up in the violet sky, the enormous surface of one of our nearby moons peeking pale over the horizon, visible even when our sun shone. I'd been used to air that carried the scent of the fields and sunlight bathing everything it touched, not the dimness of the Vandar ship and the wide view onto endless black space. Even the Zagrath ship had featured sleek, white walls and bright lights.

Peering around the sleeping chamber, I was struck by how cold it felt. Despite the bed being covered in claret-colored fabrics and piles of cushions in various hues of crimson, there was a somber feeling that hung in the air. Even the thick drapery hanging from the bed's canopy made it more claustrophobic than cozy. A fireplace inset in the obsidian wall dividing this room from the attached chamber burned, but the blue flames did not give off much heat.

Strangely, the bedroom I'd been led through on the way to this one didn't seem as cold, even though it was decorated almost entirely in black. That enormous bed held no cushions—only silky sheets, and a throw made out of something fluffy and dark-brown across the foot—but it was more appealing than the one I sat on. The thought that it was the bed where the Raas slept made my mouth go dry.

"Snap out of it, girl." I shook my head as I tried to push thoughts of the huge, tailed alien from my mind and stop the flush that threatened to creep up my neck again. I was being ridiculous. Raas Toraan was not the kind of alien to get distracted around. He was deadly and dangerous, and held my fate in his hands. I could not afford to let myself be drawn in by him—no matter how his touch made my body react.

I closed my eyes and inhaled deeply, the cool air comforting. The gentle rumbling of the massive ship's engines vibrated my feet, and the muffled sound was the only thing that kept the silence from swallowing me whole. I blew out a long breath. I needed to stay calm if I was going to pull this off.

It was true that I had information the Vandar would want. It was also true that the admiral had spoken freely in front of me on multiple occasions. None of that had been a lie. But I might have implied that I knew more than I did.

If I was being honest with myself, I hadn't always paid attention to what the admiral and his cronies babbled on about. At the time, I hadn't been too interested. Even though my memory was excellent, I did need to be focusing in order to recall details. And the details of the Zagrath plan were where I was fuzzy.

I opened my eyes and stamped one foot on the floor. Why hadn't I listened more carefully when the admiral had droned on and on about defeating the Vandar?

Because you were bored out of your mind, and you never imagined you'd ever be on an actual Vandar warbird having to barter information for sanctuary, that's why.

At least I had retained the basic information, and the broad strokes of what the admiral was up to. That had to be worth something.

And when I'd passed on everything I knew? I nibbled my bottom lip again. I couldn't lie. One look in the Raas' hazel eyes had told me he would not tolerate deception.

What surprised me was that I didn't want to lie to him. Even though my plan was to barter information, I wanted to help him.

"You're crazy," I muttered to myself. "They're Vandar. He's a Raas of the Vandar. You know what everyone says about them."

I'd heard tales about the brutal Vandar for most of my life. The scourge of the galaxy, they were violent monsters who appeared out of thin air and killed everything in their path without mercy. But that story didn't fit with the raiders I'd just met.

Sure, they were huge, and intimidating as hell, but Raas Toraan did not seem like a brute. Actually, he seemed much more disciplined and controlled than the Zagrath admiral who'd been prone to slamming his fist on the table and yelling so much that spittle would fly from his mouth. I cringed at the memory, then shuddered at the horrible thought of the old man's mouth on me.

"I'd rather die," I whispered into the quiet.

"I hope death will be unnecessary."

The deep burr made my head snap over to where the Raas stood in the doorway. How had he approached so quietly that I hadn't heard him? Or had he been there for a while, and I'd been so distracted by thinking about him that I hadn't noticed?

I stood quickly, bowing my head. I still didn't know what I was supposed to do in the presence of a Vandar warlord, and my mother's constant instruction on protocol was hard to shake. "I didn't see you there, Raas."

He grunted and stepped into the room. "You do not need to bow to me."

I looked up, but almost wished I hadn't. Raas Toraan no longer wore his shoulder armor. His chest was completely bare of straps, which made the black marks that curled across his skin even more prominent, and his muscles seem larger. His stomach was a series of sculpted ridges that disappeared beneath the wide, leather belt that hung low on his waist, and veins threaded the hard muscles of his arms. I forced myself to look anywhere but his bare skin, which meant I once again stared at the floor.

"I'm glad you are awake, but I am also pleased you were able to rest." The Raas crossed the room to stand in front of me, his feet set wide and his tail swishing slowly behind him. "Do you find the chamber comfortable?"

I hesitated before speaking. "Yes, Raas."

He reached over and put a finger under my chin, lifting my head so that I had to look him in the face. "I thought we agreed that you would not lie to me."

The deadly purr of his voice sent a shiver down my spine. "I did not mean to lie to you, Raas. The room is fine."

"But. . .?" he prodded.

"It is cold."

He turned to look at the fire. "I can see that the heat output is increased." He glanced back at me and down at my dress. "We should also get you something more suitable to wear. Do all females from your planet dress like this?"

I almost grinned at that. "No, Raas. This is my wedding dress. I was being fitted for it when the attack happened. I saw that the battle was the best opportunity for escape, so I took it. There was no time to change."

He dropped his finger from under my chin. "This is your wedding dress?"

I nodded, grabbing the layers of fabric with one hand and then letting them fall. "It's fluffier than I would have liked, but I didn't have much say in it."

Stepping back, he nodded. "I will get you warmer clothes."

I took a breath to gather my courage. "It isn't that the temperature of the room is cold. It just feels like it holds bad energy or something."

Now his eyebrows shot up. "Bad energy?"

"On Horl, we believe that objects can retain energy or memories. This room holds unhappiness, which makes it feel cold."

He studied me for a moment. "Horl sounds like an interesting planet."

My throat thickened as images of my home world rushed over me, then the realization that I would never see it again. I let my eyes drop so he wouldn't notice the tears stinging the backs of my eyes and think I was weak.

"If this room does not feel right to you, I will not make you stay here." He spun, and the leather strips that made up his short skirt slapped his thighs. He strode away from me, pausing when he'd reached the doorway. "*Vaes.*"

When I didn't respond to the Vandar word, he held out a hand. "It means 'come.'"

I hurried over to him, committing the meaning of the word to memory and taking his hand, which was surprisingly warm, considering how little clothing the guy wore. "Where will I stay?"

He pulled me into the attached bedroom and tightened his grip on my hand. "You will stay with me."

I tried to tug my hand out of his as panic fluttered in my chest. This had not been part of the plan. "I promised to give you information. Nothing else." I glanced at his enormous bed and heat pulsed between my legs. "I have no desire to warm your bed."

He shook his head slowly, the black pupils of his eyes flaring as the hazel around them shifted to green. "That's your second lie."

CHAPTER SIX

Toraan

"I do not understand, Raas." Rolan stood with his hands braced on his hips as he and Viken gathered with me in my strategy room. "How can a human female know anything of Zagrath strategy?"

"She was the admiral's bride," I said, turning to face my star chart. "He spoke about his plans in front of her."

"That is why we don't have females on Vandar warbirds," Viken muttered darkly. "They bring out weakness in warriors."

I could not disagree, although my uncle, the Raas who had trained me, had believed otherwise. The loss of his mate had been a blow that had hastened his departure from the raiders, and I'd seen it eat away at him even before he had given up his position as Raas.

"She is mated to a Zagrath admiral?" Rolan asked. "And we are keeping her on board? Are we not worried she is a spy or a saboteur?"

I attempted to focus on the points of light illuminated on the transparent, wall-sized board, but my mind was distracted by thoughts of her. Her small hand in mine, trembling even as her chest had heaved. I spun around and shook my head, dislodging the image and my *majak's* misunderstanding. "She was not mated to him. She was his intended bride, but she ran from the union. In exchange for us keeping her from him, she has offered insight into what she claims is a dedicated plan to take us down."

Rolan's face betrayed his shock. "A plan? I thought the empire only concerned itself with colonizing and ruling, so as to grow their own control and fortune."

"That is true," I said. "But Rachael claims that this admiral is not satisfied to only battle us when we thwart their overreach."

"Rachael?"

I twitched one shoulder as if this was nothing. "That is her name. She is from a human colony on Horl."

Viken frowned. "Human names are unusual, as are the small creatures themselves."

Rolan moved his hands behind his back and clasped them. "And what has this human called Rachael revealed so far? What details of the plan has she told you?"

I hated to admit that so far she had told me nothing. It was not that she had withheld the information. I had been so distracted by the desire I'd read on her face that I'd backed away and come to join my officers on the command deck. Here, in my strategy room, where we planned battles and mapped out long-term campaigns, I felt calm. Nothing like the jangle of nerves I'd experienced being close to her.

The last time I'd been so affected by a female, I'd gone into a destructive spiral that had taken many bloody battles for me to pull myself out. I did not want to experience that again, no matter how beautiful and appealing I found the human.

"I am working on extracting the intelligence," I said, pivoting back to the star chart so they would not see the conflict on my face. "It must be done delicately. This human female is not like a Garunthian, who will spill everything if you threaten to cut off their tentacles."

"Too bad," Viken grumbled.

"Forget the female." I tapped a finger on the clear chart. "Before we were drawn to this sector by the other horde, we'd been observing unusual movements by imperial ships. Maybe that movement and the information the female has are related."

Rolan joined me at the star chart, peering at the glowing lines that traced the movement of the enemy fleet. "It is possible."

Viken growled low. "I still say we do not know for sure if this female is a spy or not. There is a chance that the enemy sent her off in a transport to draw our interest. I am not convinced she isn't a plant who's been given false information to feed us."

My first instinct was to snap at my battle chief and defend Rachael. I believed her story. I'd seen the fear and disgust in her eyes when she'd talked about the imperial admiral. But I could not discount my warrior's doubt. He was right to be wary. We knew nothing of the human, but we knew a great deal about how ruthless our enemy was. They would think nothing of sacrificing a female for their own gain. And she might be a spy without even knowing it.

"We should consider what Viken says." My *majak* did not look over at me when he spoke, but his meaning was clear. *I needed to be more cautious with the information I gathered.*

"Agreed." I thumped my *majak* on the back. "Do not worry that I have gone soft, Rolan. I am still the Raas who has out-strategized the enemy every step of the way."

"I do not think we *shouldn't* listen to the human." Viken stepped up to the star chart, leaning one hand on the smooth surface. "But we should authenticate her story."

I twisted my head to him. "We cannot reveal that we have her."

He shook his head, and his hair swung around his scruffy cheeks. "No, but if she truly escaped would they not search for her, or send out messages to other imperial ships? This may not be a love match, but I suspect the admiral paid well for his bride. He will want to retake his property."

A growl escaped my throat. "A Zagrath does not deserve her."

"A Zagrath deserves nothing but death," Viken added.

"A Vandar has never taken something of such value to the empire before," Rolan said. "If she truly ran from her union to an admiral, our possession of her is already a blow to them."

Viken let out a low chuckle. "Imagine the admiral's humiliation at his bride running out on him."

Rolan elbowed me. "Imagine how much worse it would be if he knew she'd taken refuge with a Vandar horde."

"If word got out that she'd chosen a warbird filled with brutes like us instead of the civilized empire," Rolan's voice became a rumble. "The admiral's humiliation would be known throughout the galaxy."

"Which is why he must not know," I said sharply. "I do not trust a Zagrath not to desire revenge for such a slight."

Both warriors grumbled, the thought of humiliating the enemy hard to give up so easily.

"Raas," my *majak* said. "We cannot keep her forever. Even if she is not a spy and provides us with valuable information, she cannot live on a Vandar warbird. She will have to leave us at some point."

I knew the wisdom of his words, but I did not agree. The only way to keep her from the admiral was to keep her on board. A female as beautiful as her could not go anywhere unnoticed. There was no colony or outpost where her startling beauty would not draw attention, and there were few places untouched by the empire. If I suspected correctly, Rachael was now the most wanted female in the galaxy.

"I have a plan that could protect her from the empire permanently," I said, even as the plan coalesced in my mind, "but I do not know if she will agree to it."

Or if it was something that would not destroy me in the process.

"She will have no choice," Viken said. "You are Raas, and on this ship, your word is law."

I drew in a long breath before the words spilled from my mouth, shocking me almost as much as they did my warriors. "She must have a choice, if she is to form mating marks with me."

CHAPTER SEVEN

Admiral Kurmog slammed his hand on the surface of his desk. "What do you mean, she's gone?"

The officer standing in front of him flinched visibly, his shoulders shrinking back even as his feet remained rooted to the floor. "We have been unable to locate her on the ship, Admiral. She was in the middle of a session with the tailor when the battle broke out. She excused herself, and never returned."

The admiral dragged a bony hand over the slick surface of his head. "Perhaps the noise of the attack scared her. She is a female, after all, and this is her first time off her backward planet."

"That is what we thought, but we have searched everywhere."

Kurmog braced his hands on the surface of his gleaming, white desk. "Are you telling me that my bride vanished into thin air?" He narrowed his eyes. "We're on a battleship. She has to be here somewhere."

The officer cleared his throat, hesitant to speak the next words. "Not necessarily. In the chaos of the battle, an unauthorized transport left our ship."

The admiral let out a derisive laugh. "You think my human bride—who had never been inside a space vessel before I plucked her from Horl—managed to pilot a transport off a battleship during a battle?"

"It is the only logical explanation."

Kurmog strode from behind his desk to the wide glass wall overlooking space. "It's preposterous. The female is known for her great beauty, not for her intelligence. And like I said, she knows nothing of space travel. She wouldn't have the first idea how to even engage a ship's engines, much less pilot it."

The officer was silent as the admiral rocked back on his heels, staring into the darkness. The admiral was in a foul mood, and this wasn't helping. Their fleet had been beaten back by the Vandar, and they'd been forced to abandon their mines on Carlogia Prime. The battle had been arduous, and their ship had taken severe damage. They'd been forced to retreat to make repairs and that was when the admiral had noticed that his fiancé was not in her quarters. He'd called for a ship-wide search, which had turned up nothing but a missing transport ship.

The admiral spun around. "Let's say she miraculously learned to pilot a vessel and managed to fly it off the battleship." The sneer on his face showed that he still thought this idea to be ludicrous. "Where is the ship now? Transports are not capable of light speed."

The officer clasped his own hands behind his back. "There are a few possibilities, sir." He drew in a breath. "She could have found a planet to hide behind—perhaps even Carlogia Prime.

We know she didn't go to the surface of that planet, though. We were monitoring all traffic during the battle, and a transport heading to the surface would have been noticed and most likely picked off by the Vandar."

Kurmog ground his teeth together at the mention of the enemy. "If they killed my bride, I will be very upset."

"We do not believe the transport was destroyed. One of our fighter pilots thinks he spotted it flying away from the planet and the battle."

"Thinks?"

The officer cleared his throat. "The battle was chaotic, sir. He cannot be certain."

Kurmog muttered a few curses under his breath. "Let us assume he is correct. My bride flew away from the battle." He swept an arm wide, waving it at the glass overlooking space. "Where is she now? Surely, our long-range sensors can detect her? As long as our transport is flying, it should be transmitting an imperial signal."

The officer's gaze went to his feet. "The signal disappeared, sir."

"Disappeared?" The admiral's voice was barely audible. "Unless the ship was blown out of the sky, or is floating dead in the water, it is impossible for it to vanish."

"Not if the transport was taken on board by another ship."

Silence stretched between the two Zagrath.

"Do you mean the Vandar?"

The raspy sound of the admiral's voice made the officer shiver and hesitate to meet his cold eyes. "It is possible that one of their hordes took the transport while they were using their invisibility shielding." The words spilled from the officer, as if saying them fast would lessen their blow. "We would not be able to track our ship if it was disengaged and on a cloaked warbird."

Kurmog walked slowly to stand behind his desk. He sat and steepled his fingers together. "Do you think this is what happened? You believe my human bride stole a transport and flew it away from this battleship into the arms of a waiting Vandar horde?"

"I would not put it like that, Admiral. I doubt the human knew she was flying into a horde."

Kurmog tapped his fingers together rhythmically. "It is true that the Vandar sent more than one horde to battle us over Carlogia Prime, and it is also true that the cowards are fond of hiding in their invisible ships." He laced his fingers, squeezing them until his knuckles were white. "If the Vandar have taken my bride, they will pay for it in blood."

"Yes, Admiral."

Kurmog stood and began to pace behind his desk. "It is clear that my bride was taken by force by the bloodthirsty and vengeful raiders as repayment for the many deaths I have bestowed upon them. This was obviously a plot by desperate brutes bent on striking a blow to me and to the empire."

The officer opened his mouth, then thought better of it and clamped it shut. "Yes, Admiral."

"An attack on my bride is an attack on me, and the empire, and we cannot let it stand." Admiral Kurmog's voice rose as he paced faster. "If they think they can take the female from me and not feel the full retribution of the empire, they are sorely mistaken. We will track my bride to the ends of the galaxy and hunt down the criminals who have snatched her from me. This insult will not go unpunished!"

"Does this mean we are changing our course, sir? Are we no longer joining the fleet at the outpost on Moravia II?"

The admiral flapped a hand dismissively. "Moravia II does not matter. The Vandar are the threat that continues to endanger the empire." He pivoted to face the officer. "Send a transmission on all channels. I want the Vandar to know that we are coming for them."

"Yes, Admiral." The officer paused. "But how will we find ships that fly unseen?"

Kurmog smiled, his lips stretching across his wrinkled face. "We will draw them out. If it is true the raiders have secret colonies where they hide their people, then we will find those. Then all the hordes will come in a futile attempt to stop me from doing what we should have done centuries ago—exterminate their species."

Chills went through the officer as he gave a sharp salute and left the admiral's ready room. If the pretty human really had gotten away from Kurmog, part of him hoped they never found her.

CHAPTER EIGHT

Rachael

I rubbed my fingers across the coarse, brown fabric that almost reached my knees. The skirt had clearly been designed for someone taller than me, but I was so grateful to get out of my pinned-together wedding dress that I didn't care what I changed into. The top was also roomy, but I'd tied the long hem up into a knot, so it didn't blouse over the skirt. That meant I showed a strip of bare stomach, but I doubted the Raas would care, since he walked around with almost nothing covering his bare chest.

Raas Toraan had been true to his word, even though I had been less than honest with him. He'd sent clothes for me, as well as an impressive spread of food that now stretched across the ebony dining table, pewter domes covering the dishes to keep them warm. Even covered, the savory scents reached my nose, and made my stomach rumble.

I might be hungry, but I didn't dare eat. The Vandar attendant who'd delivered the clothes and food—and who looked to be no more than a mere boy—had told me that Raas Toraan would be returning to his quarters to join me for dinner. I still wasn't sure about Vandar protocol, but I was pretty sure that devouring a warlord's dinner would be considered bad form. And as much as I hated hearing my mother's instruction in my head all the time, I was nothing, if not well-trained in etiquette.

Protocol was one of the few things my mother had thought I needed to learn. I'd been endlessly drilled on how to eat, curtsy, and simper—skills she believed I'd need as the wife of someone important.

"Because selling me off to the highest bidder was always the plan," I muttered bitterly to myself. Part of me hoped my parents were told that I was missing, and an even darker part of me wished they knew I was not married to the admiral, but was on a Vandar ship. I got a perverse sense of pleasure imagining my mother's shocked face, if she knew I was in the sleeping chamber of a raider warlord. I could almost see her thin lips pursed in prim disapproval.

She'd worn that look of distaste when she'd been helping me pack to leave my home and join the admiral on his ship. It wasn't my leaving, or the admiral, who provoked her disapproved. It was the last bit of instruction she felt she needed to impart to me that made her lips pucker and her brow furrow.

"It's your duty as a wife to submit," she'd said tightly. "Whatever he wants, even if it's unpleasant, or you don't wish it."

I'd kept my face averted from her, my nod the only response. She believed she was giving sage advice to a virgin, that I had no idea what to expect from the marriage bed. It would have been a good assumption. She and my father had made sure none of my suitors had spent any time alone with me, and none of the local boys had been allowed near our mansion. Even at dances, my mother had watched me like a Horlian hawk.

But I'd known her and my father's plan. I'd heard them talking about the admiral. I'd also picked up that he was not a young man, but my mother's initial objection to his age and appearance had been silenced by my father.

I might not have had any power over my life, or have gotten to pick my husband, but I wasn't about to have my first time be with some decrepit old Zagrath. My parents might keep out the other well-bred boys on Horl, but they did not think of the horse master's assistant, who spent as much time in the stables as I did. It probably never occurred to them that I would take him up to the stable loft and ask him to fuck me, promising him that I would never breathe a word of it, and assuring him that he would not lose his job.

I smiled as I thought back to our hurried coupling—his movements at first tentative and unsure, as if he wasn't convinced I'd meant what I'd said. My initial yelp of pain had startled him, but I'd urged him on, craving his urgent thrusts. It hadn't lasted long, and he'd pulled out at the last second, spilling his seed on my thigh and then collapsing next to me. He'd heaved in uneven breaths for a while, before apologizing for being so fast and asking if we could do it again. I'd eagerly agreed, knowing the dark-haired boy was my last chance, and I'd savored my afternoon in the hayloft with him thrusting eagerly between my legs.

So, when my mother had started in on her droning instruction about pleasing a male by lying prone and quiet, I'd tuned her out and smiled at my own memories of riding the horse master's assistant until I'd had to hold my hands over his mouth to keep his screams from carrying out of the barn. I hadn't loved him, or even known him very well, but he'd been sweet and attentive, and hell-bent on pleasing me in as many positions as possible. And by fucking him until I could barely walk, I'd taken something from the old man who thought he was buying a beautiful virgin. He would never be my first, and I would always know that I'd chosen a stable boy over him. A boy whose hair smelled of fresh hay and who would never command anything greater than a stable.

"Take that, asshole," I whispered, smiling at my remembered rebellion.

"I hope that was not meant for me."

Once again, Raas Toraan had entered the room without me noticing, although to be fair, I had been completely immersed in my memories.

"No," I answered quickly. "I was thinking about… someone else."

He nodded as he crossed to me without removing his shoulder armor. "I apologize for leaving so abruptly earlier. I needed to attend to matters on my command deck." His gaze slid over me then returned to my face. "You received the clothes, I see."

"Yes, thank you. They're much more comfortable than a wedding dress filled with straight pins."

His eyes lingered on me for a beat then he turned to the table and waved a hand at the benches on either side. "Sit."

I took a seat on one side of the table and he took the bench on the other side, lifting domes off the plates and drawing in a deep breath. Although I had a metal plate in front of me, there was no silverware, so I watched as Raas Toraan served us both, then ripped small wedges of flat bread and started scooping the food with them. I followed suit, making triangular pockets of bread to hold chunks of the stew-like dishes.

After a few bites, I eagerly drank from my goblet. The food had strong flavors with unusual spices, and I was grateful for the kick of the wine to wash it away. The wine had its own different kind of kick, though, and I suspected I shouldn't drink too much of it.

The Raas ate quickly, tossing back a full goblet of wine and then refilling it and downing that, as well. If I didn't know that he was a Vandar warrior, I would have thought he was nervous. But why would a raider warlord be nervous? Maybe it wasn't nerves, but agitation. Was he irritated at me because I hadn't revealed any of the information I'd promised? I did not want the one person who could keep me from the admiral's clutches to think I wasn't holding up my end of the bargain.

He sat back, his gaze focused on me. "Rachael, I have— "

"It's okay," I said, cutting him off before he could tell me that he'd changed his mind about keeping me from the empire. "I'm ready."

"What?"

"I'm ready to tell you what I know about the Zagrath plans. Isn't that what you want?"

The Raas straightened, taking another gulp of wine and dragging the back of his hand across his mouth. "Of course."

I followed his lead and took a sip of wine. "I didn't always pay attention to what the admiral said to his officers. He did talk a lot, and most of it was boring."

The Raas inclined his head as if telling me to continue.

"But he did seem obsessed with you guys, the Vandar, that is. He's convinced you're hiding some big secret, and if he finds that then he'll be able to wipe you all out for good."

The Raas went still. "Secret?"

"I know. It's a little crazy-sounding, but Kurmog thinks you have colonies of your people stashed someplace so the empire can't find them. He told his officers that he wants to find them and finish what the Zagrath should have a long time ago."

Toraan stood so quickly he bumped the table, and the dishes and goblets shook from the impact. His jaw was tight, and his pupils had widened so that his eyes looked almost black.

"Are you okay? Did I say something wrong?"

He gave his head a brusque shake. "Thank you for the meal and the information. I need to return to my command deck."

"So, you won't turn me over to the empire?" I asked as he walked to the door.

His gaze held me as he pressed his hand to a panel and the arched door slid open. "I have no intention of giving you to the empire—not now and not ever. You belong to the Vandar."

CHAPTER 9

Toraan

I stormed through the ship, my heart hammering as relentlessly as my boots pounding the floor. The Zagrath knew about our colonies? It was impossible. We'd kept them secret for centuries, protecting the last of our people from the reach of our enemy. The only thought that kept me from breaking into a run was that they did not know the locations. Without the coordinates, the imperial admiral had nothing but suspicions.

"Which is how it will stay," I growled, as I reached my destination.

Stepping into the warriors' canteen, I raked my eyes across the narrow room until I spotted my *majak*. Rolan leaned against the long, iron bar with a glass of murky, green liquid in one hand. Karvolian gin. A sure indicator my most trusted officer was drinking the day's events away, much as I wished to do.

Heads swiveled and heels clicked together in salute as warriors spotted me. I did not often join in the drinking after a shift, preferring to pore over star charts and revise strategy, but my presence was also not completely unusual. I nodded to acknowledge the salutes and made my way to Rolan.

He straightened as I approached. "Raas?" The word was both a greeting and a question. He knew I'd gone to dine with the human female, and yet here I was, not long after I'd left him.

"*Zaiva*," I said, loud enough for all the warriors around me to hear the Vandar word for "at ease" and go back to their drinking without fear of committing offense. Then I waved for the Vandar pouring drinks and pointed to my *majak's* glass. "Another one."

"I take it your suggestion was not taken well?" Rolan asked.

I'd almost forgotten my plan to claim the female and give her mating marks, although the thought of it now made my pulse quicken and my cock twitch. "I did not bring it up."

I lifted the glass of Karvolian gin that was poured for me, and took a long drink of the bitter liquid. I welcomed the burn that scorched my throat, and instantly numbed my frantic thoughts. "But she did share some intelligence with me."

Rolan remained silent, his gaze locked on me. One of his great skills as a *majak* was his patience.

I let my voice drop and leaned my head close to his. "She says the Zagrath admiral knows about our colonies. At least, he thinks he does."

Although he didn't respond, I noticed a muscle tick in his jaw.

"He does not know locations or coordinates, so his suspicions are just that."

Rolan took a drink of his own gin. "Do you believe her?"

"I believe that is what the admiral said. Otherwise, how would a human female from Horl know anything about the colonies, or even about us?"

Rolan nodded slowly, as if acknowledging the truth in my logical assumption. "That does not rule out this information being fed to her intentionally. If she is a spy, this could be what they want us to think."

Irritation flared within me at the suggestion that she was working for the enemy. Rolan had not looked into her eyes and seen the fear in them. No, she had escaped from the empire because she was running from someone and something she couldn't bear.

Then again, I could not fully discount the possibility that she was being used by our enemy. They were sinister enough to use a female as bait and not think twice, even a female engaged to an admiral. I would not have been surprised to discover that the Zagrath admiral had sacrificed her himself. "If she is a spy, she is an unwitting one. She believes every word she told me."

My *majak* inclined his head at me. We'd both been trained by my uncle in the art of detecting deception. It was one of the many reasons we trusted each other with our lives. We were both too skilled at sensing lies to ever deceive each other. Then again, I'd been fooled by a female before, and knew better than to let my head be clouded by one so intriguing.

I slammed back what was left of my drink. "I do not believe the Zagrath let her go. The admiral paid too much for her." I did not add that she was too beautiful to be relinquished, unless the admiral no longer felt the hot rush of desire.

"There you are." Viken's voice made us both turn, as he pushed through the growing crush of warriors to join us, his face set in a scowl.

"What is it?" Rolan asked when my battle chief reached us.

"I went to your quarters, Raas." His face flushed. "The human said you had rushed out."

I peered into my empty glass. "She shared unsettling information." I jerked my head toward Rolan. "We are trying to determine if it is valid, or if she is being used by the empire to scare us into a false move."

"I know I suggested she was sent by the empire as a spy." Viken jutted his chin up. "I no longer believe that."

"What changed your thinking?" Rolan asked, waving for the bartender to refill our drinks and serve one to Viken. "Did the female make that strong of an impression on you just now?"

My battle chief cut his eyes to my *majak*, reminding me that the two Vandar were half-brothers and naturally competitive, although different in almost every way. "I came from the command deck. We intercepted a transmission the Zagrath admiral is sending out on all frequencies."

"A transmission?" I asked.

He pressed his lips together briefly. "A threat, Raas."

"The Zagrath admiral is issuing a threat?" My heart beat faster. "About the female?"

"Affirmative." Viken picked up the glass of Karvolian gin in front of him. "He is issuing a claim on the human as his property, and promises death to any Vandar who touches her. He demands she be returned to him unharmed, and promises war if she is not."

Rolan's eyebrows lifted. "Then they know we have her."

"Who else could have taken her?" I said. "Only Vandar and Zagrath were near the battle at Carlogia Prime. It's the logical conclusion."

"There is more, Raas." Viken's frown deepened. "The transmission says that if we keep the female, we will pay in the lives of those we've hidden."

My skin went cold as Rolan froze next to me.

Viken pounded a fist on the bar. "How could they know, Raas?"

"That is the information the female shared with me." I gazed into the murky green contents of my drink. "The admiral knows of the existence of our colonies, but does not know where."

Viken's mouth dropped. "How?"

"We do not know." Rolan cast his eyes around the room. "We all guard the secret with our lives. Every warrior in this horde has family in the colonies. It could not have come from any Vandar."

Viken slammed back a gulp of gin. "We should contact the other hordes. Your brothers might know how this happened."

I shook my head hard. "Not yet. I don't want to panic the hordes." And I did not want to explain to my brothers that I was getting intelligence from a human female, despite the fact that my eldest brother had taken a human mate. "We will wait until we know more."

Viken did not look pleased with my response, but he did not challenge it. He knew I would always do what was best for the horde, and for the Vandar.

"What will you do Raas?" Rolan asked.

"We do not do the empire's bidding." I took a gulp of gin, the searing heat fueling the fire that burned in my belly. "They cannot scare us into giving away what we have taken. Raiders do not give. We take. We are Vandar."

Viken emitted a rumble. "We are Vandar."

"The admiral does not know how to find our colonies, and he does not know how to find us," I continued. "Like the old man himself, his bark has no teeth. We will not return the human. It is done."

I tossed back the rest of my gin, and it scorched a trail down my throat.

"Where are you going Raas?" Rolan asked as I turned to leave.

I thought of my destination, and my cock swelled. "To compel the female to tell me everything she knows."

CHAPTER 10

I don't know when I fell asleep, but I woke with the Raas staring at me. He sat on an ottoman near the bed, resting his elbows on his knees. He no longer wore the straps crossing his chest, and his stomach muscles rippled as he bent forward, his long dark hair falling over his shoulders.

The lights in the room were dimmer than they had been, the crackling blue flames inset in the wall giving off most of the light. I sat up. "Is it morning? How long have I been asleep?"

He tilted his head. "There is no morning on a spaceship. Only first watch. But no, you did not sleep long."

That explained why I felt so groggy. I hadn't slept well since I'd left my home planet, and the stress of the escape and being taken onto a Vandar warbird was catching up to me.

I glanced down. I was still fully dressed. I remembered thinking that I would just lie on the bed for a minute as I waited for the Raas to return, but the bed had been so soft and the sheets so silky that I'd closed my eyes and let my mind wander.

I focused on the warlord watching me, the shadows cast on his face making him look even more intimidating than usual. I thought back to what I'd told him about the admiral, and how he'd left in a rush. "Is everything okay? Am…am I in trouble?"

Toraan entwined his fingers. "Why would you be in trouble?"

At home I could get reprimanded for laughing too loudly or speaking out of turn or scraping my spoon across the bottom of my soup bowl. I suspected the Vandar didn't consider any of these things punishable offenses. I shrugged. "I don't know, but you look pretty serious."

He blew out a breath and stood quickly. "The admiral knows we have you."

My stomach clenched. "What? How? I thought your horde was invisible?"

"It is. He cannot know where you are, or which horde has taken possession of you, but he has surmised that you are with the Vandar."

I swung my legs over the side of the bed, the cold floor a shock to my bare feet. "How do you know this?"

The Raas stood with his legs wide and his hands behind his back, his tail almost motionless as it curved up behind him. "Kurmog has sent out a transmission threatening war against any Vandar who dares keep you."

Bile churned in my stomach, and I tasted it in the back of my throat. I couldn't go back to him. The thought of the old man's cold, bony hands on me, and his papery lips on mine, made me want to scream. I didn't care what deal my parents had made, or what I'd agreed to when I'd joined his ship. I refused to be some imperial breeder for a male with dead eyes and a hard heart.

I wrapped my arms around my stomach and bent over, letting out a small moan. "Please don't send me back to him. Let me go in the imperial transport, and I won't tell a soul that I was ever on your ship."

He took a step closer to me. "I have no intention of returning you to the empire."

I tipped my head back to peer up at him. "You don't?"

Another cock of his head. "You think a Raas of the Vandar is afraid of imperial threats?"

I sucked in a cool breath, my stomach relaxing. "You'd risk war with the empire for someone you don't even know?"

"We are Vandar." His lips quirked up on one side. "We welcome battle with the Zagrath. We do not run from it. And I would never do your admiral's bidding."

"He's not my admiral," I grumbled. "I don't ever want to see him for as long as I live."

"Then you are certain you do not wish to marry him? You will not change your mind?"

I laughed and gave him a look that told him I thought he was insane to even ask me. "I had nothing to do with setting up the sham marriage. My parents claimed they were making a great match for me, but it was really for them." My eyes burned with tears. "What kind of parents make their only daughter marry a man three times her age?"

"If you are sure you do not want to return to him or the empire, you do not have to marry him. I will hide you. But you can also never return to your home world, or leave the Vandar. Do you understand?"

I hesitated for only a moment. I loved Horl, but not as much as I despised the thought of being married to the admiral. Even though it was hard to imagine spending my life with a Vandar horde, it beat the alternative. "I understand."

The Raas nodded solemnly and turned, taking long steps to stand at the gleaming black wall that contained the fireplace. He leaned one hand on the wall above the dancing flames and gazed at them. His shoulders were bunched with tension, and the tip of his tail flicked rapidly.

"Does this mean that the empire will be hunting for me?" I asked.

He nodded without turning.

"And they might take their anger out on your people?"

He gave a rough shake of his head. "They would have to find us first, and the empire does not yet know how to find a hidden horde."

"What about the colonies that the admiral mentioned?" I asked. "If that's where the rest of the Vandar live, will keeping me put them in danger?"

The hand on the wall curled into a fist. "They will never find them."

I didn't want to argue with him, but I'd seen the steely determination on the admiral's face. He would not give up—especially now. I stood and walked to the fire. "I know the Vandar love battle, but why would you do this for me? You don't get anything but a target on your back in return."

He twisted his head to meet my eyes. The light of the flames cavorted across his face, making his handsome features appear fierce. "That does not have to be true."

My pulse skittered as his gaze held mine. "I don't under—"

"Do you wish to strike a blow against the admiral himself? Do you want to ensure he will never want to reclaim you as his bride?"

I nodded without hesitation. I despised the man and the way he'd looked at me, as if I was his property.

His eyes darkened as he spoke, his voice a velvet purr. "If you become a Raisa of the Vandar, you will render yourself untouchable."

A breath caught in my throat. "A Raisa? What does that mean."

The Raas closed the small distance between us, his body almost flush with mine. "The mate of a Raas. A Raisa takes the mating marks of her Raas."

My gaze went to the curls that inked his chest. "I would get tattoos?"

He took my hand in his and touched it to one of the dark swirls. "These are not tattoos. Vandar are born with these marks, and when we take our mate, they appear on her skin, as well."

I swallowed hard, his skin hot beneath my fingers. "You want me to…?"

"If you wear my marks, no Zagrath would touch you. You would be safe."

As I stared into his molten gaze, safe wasn't the word that came to mind. "And it would prove to the admiral that I don't belong to him?"

He inclined his head to me. "It would."

I liked the sound of *that*, but was I ready to run from one male's arms right into another? I'd finally gotten out from under my parents' control. Did I really want to give up my power so quickly?

I swallowed hard. "Are you serious? You barely know me."

He cocked one eyebrow. "What else should I know about you?"

I opened my mouth to answer then clamped it shut. This clearly wasn't some sort of love match for him. I'd never been a helpless romantic, but I'd always imagined a husband would be a little more excited than *this*. "Nothing, I guess. You're sure you want to do this just to keep me safe from the empire? You aren't supposed to do this with a Vandar female, instead?"

"A Vandar mate has never been in the cards for me." He looked into the fire briefly, then back at me, his face set in determination. "Striking a blow against the Zagrath is reason enough."

A part of me knew it was foolish to go from one captor to another, but another part didn't care, as long as I never had to be married to the admiral. "I…I don't know."

His profile was even more stark in the dancing flames of the fire as he scowled at me. "You do not know if you wish to be honored as the mate of a Vandar Raas?" The Raas' tail curled around the back of my legs and a shiver of unexpected desire slid down my spine. "I think you do know."

CHAPTER 11

Toraan

"It's only to protect her." I dodged the holographic axe blade as it sliced the air, and my shoulder hit the curved metal wall.

Viken dashed in front of me and lifted his battle axe high to block the next attack. "I do not understand, Raas."

I pushed myself off the wall of the holographic battle ring and sucked in a hot breath. Sweat trickled down my chest, and I swiped a hand across my slick brow, never taking my eyes off the holographic beast we were battling. Although we were in a long, cylindrical chamber used for battle practice, the creature growling at us was one hundred percent energy, and covered with thick, matted fur best suited for a glacier planet.

"The only way to ensure that the admiral will not claim the female is for her to have Vandar mating marks," I said, my tail swishing behind me as I pivoted.

Viken let out a choked laugh. "You are right about that. No Zagrath would take a mate who has been marked by a Vandar."

He spun around to watch for incoming strikes, crouched in a battle stance and shifting his weight from one foot to another as the tip of his tail quivered in anticipation. "But she is a human, Raas."

"Do you think I do not know that?" Before, I would have thought it impossible that a Vandar could share mating marks with a human, but word had spread through the hordes that my eldest brother, Kratos, had formed mating marks with the human female he'd taken as his captive. There were whispers that she even dressed like a Vandar warrior. My mind wandered to the image of Rachael dressed in a battle kilt with her brown skin exposed, and my cock twitched.

I growled and ignored the heat coiling in my belly. I needed to think of something other than the human waiting for me in my quarters. I lunged at the holo-beast, my blade catching in his fur but not doing any damage.

Kaalek. The image of my other older brother dampened my desire instantly. He had also taken a female onboard his ship, although I had not heard if they were mates or shared marks yet. It had not happened often, but there was now evidence that it was possible for Vandar and human to share markings. It would not be a stretch to think it could happen for me.

Before I could say all this to my battle chief, he rolled across the mat and leapt to his feet across from me. "And how can you be sure that she will take your marks, if this is just part of a strategy?"

I did not want to admit that my body heated with longing when I looked at her, or that the thought of the human having my marks etched on her skin made my long-dormant heart stir. "I cannot know for sure, but it is worth the risk."

Viken grunted in response as we both brought our blades crashing down on the towering, holographic beast. My axe vibrated from the contact, and for a moment, I regretted setting the program to its most challenging setting. Then again, it had been a while since I'd fought off Turmerian ice trolls—real or holographic—and my body welcomed the release.

We both jumped back and watched the shimmering opponent swing his spiked mace. Even though our advanced holographic technology—the same tech that we used in our invisibility shielding—meant that the image was comprised of energy, the blows still hurt, and the wounds were still real.

"This is not just to strike the imperial admiral where it will hurt him most?" Viken asked, over the roar of the ice troll as it thundered toward us.

I dipped low and slashed at the creature's legs, taking off one enormous, fur-covered foot. "Can it not be both?"

Viken laughed as he dashed forward, swinging himself up onto the troll's back. "As long as you are sure, Raas." He slashed at the creature's wide throat, causing dark blood to stain the matted white fur before the image flickered and then vanished. Falling from high in the air, my battle chief landed in a crouch. Since the opponent had been killed, the program had ended.

I was not sorry. It was our third holo-battle, and we'd already defeated a giant Crelibri slug and a Protorian boar. I strode forward and clapped him on the shoulder. "Well done."

He grinned, heaving in a breath. "Your blow to his legs made my death blow possible."

"Battles are always won together," I said, echoing something my uncle had repeated often. It was a core tenet of the horde. We fought and won together. There were no individual victories for the Vandar.

"Another?" He tossed the handle of his axe from hand to hand.

I shook my head. "It is enough for now."

"No sand scorpion today?"

I laughed. He knew how I despised battling the creature with snapping pincers. "You will have to face that on your own."

Viken looked at me as we both leaned on our battle axes and caught our breath. I cocked my head at him. "I know that look. You are concerned about something."

"I had thought you'd abandoned any goal of taking a mate."

My gut clenched, even as I tried to force the memories from my mind. "That was long ago."

"True, but you'd thought she was your one true mate." Viken had served with me long enough to know everything about me, which could be a curse.

Images of the Vandar female I'd been sure would take my mating marks flooded my brain, even as I tried to shake them off. Like all Vandar, Lila had dark hair, and she'd worn hers pulled on top of her head in a sleek bun that had made her long-lashed eyes even more striking. "We were young. I was foolish."

"You were deceived, Raas." His voice was steady, but held bitterness I rarely heard from him.

"It is done." I huffed out a breath. "We did not have more than a childhood promise. She never wore my marks."

Viken muttered darkly under his breath. He knew that I had shared a bond with the female, and many nights. His loyalty to me—and therefore his disdain for the female who had rejected me—was absolute. "And this is not about taking revenge against her."

Irritation flared in my chest. "I would not use one female to exact penance on another."

Viken shrugged. "I would not blame you for wanting Lila to see you mated with another, Raas. And a human mate as beautiful as the one in your quarters would show her that she had not broken you."

I leveled my gaze at my battle chief. "You believe me broken?"

"No, Raas," he said quickly.

I was not sure that I believed him, or that he was entirely wrong. I had skillfully avoided any contact with Vandar females —not difficult on a horde ship—or any thought of mates. When other raiders had returned to the Vandar colonies to take mates, I'd wished them well but never felt even a twinge of jealousy. That part of myself had been closed off forever. Until now.

"I promise you this agreement is only about protecting the female and keeping her from the admiral's reach, while striking a blow to the empire at the same time. I am in no danger of losing my heart again."

He nodded, but the expression on his face told me he remembered how I'd been when I'd returned to the colonies and discovered Lila was mated to another. It had been a dark time in my past, punctuated by long sessions in the battle ring, many with Viken.

I grasped his forearm and held his gaze with mine. "I assure you. This is different. I am going into this arrangement with a clear understanding on both sides. The female has her reasons, and so do I. Emotional attachment is not one of them for either of us."

Even as I attempted to convince my fellow warrior, the words sounded hollow to my ears. My idea was impulsive and unlike my usually measured strategy. Yes, taking Rachael as a mate could be seen as strategy, but it was one with an outcome that could not be assured. My uncle and mentor would have called it reckless, and I suspected he would have been right. Even though Rachael had not given me an answer, thoughts of her were crowding my mind, and proving to be a distraction I did not need.

Was I trying to use her as a salve for my residual longing for Lila? Was it possible to erase the pain of a lost love with a new one? If it was, that was one more reason to take Rachael as a mate. Even though my heartache had faded over time, the memories still haunted me, and I wished to banish them once and for all.

We headed for the exit of the holo-ring, but before I could press my hand to the door panel, the ship shuddered and lurched forward. I stumbled into the wall with Viken beside me.

"*Tvek!*" I said, a jolt of pain shooting up my arm from the impact.

"What was that?"

I held my palms to the cool steel of the wall. "The ship has stopped."

Viken didn't move for a moment, as he also listened for the familiar burr of the engines. "You're right."

"The Zagrath," we both said, at once.

"They can't have found us," I said, more to convince myself than Viken. "The enemy does not possess the technology."

But what else could it be? I pressed my hand to open the door and ran for the command deck with my battle chief by my side. And what else could they be after, but the female I intended to claim as my own?

CHAPTER 12

Toraan

"Report!" I bellowed, as Viken and I stormed the command deck. We'd raced up from the bowels of the ship where the holo-ring was located, and sweat still beaded our bodies.

Rolan stood at his console, his arms gripping the edges. He tapped his heels together as he turned. "It's a blockade, Raas."

I shifted my focus to the wide view screen. What appeared to be a wall of gray Zagrath ships stretched out in front of us. Not all were bulky battleships, but there were enough of the blocky vessels that my stomach sank. While my horde was the largest of all Vandar hordes—and equipped with the most sophisticated weaponry—we were no match for this. Not alone.

"*Tvek*," I muttered as Viken strode to his station.

I braced my feet wide and overlooked both the command deck and the view screen. Unlike most ships, my command deck did not have a captain's chair. Vandar Raas' did not sit while they commanded, just as our warriors did not sit at their stations. We needed to be prepared to fight at any moment, and sitting did not give a strategic advantage.

Viken swiped his fingers across his console. "They can't know we're here."

Rolan gave a single shake of his head. "If my suspicions are correct, this is not their only blockade."

"They're trying to set up a net so they can catch us," I said.

"Or catch the female," Viken added.

The hard lump in my gut hardened into a cold ball. The admiral was intent in his desire to find Rachael. More than I'd expected he would be.

He could not love her. Rachael had all but told me they'd had no intimate contact and few conversations. But he clearly believed her to be his, and it seemed he was willing to go to great lengths to retrieve her.

"Orders, Raas?" Viken's hand hovered over his controls. He was itching to fire at our enemy.

My own fingers tingled with the desire for battle, but I steadied my breath. Rushing in from the battle ring had put me on edge, but once we fired, our horde would be revealed, and our tactical advantage gone.

"Hold fire." I bit out the words. "If they do not know we are here, let's not give ourselves away."

"You wish to wait?" Rolan asked. "Should we summon another horde? Your brothers can't be too far away."

"No," The words came out sharper than I'd intended. "The empire wants us to fire. That's why they're here—to draw us into a battle so they can weaken us. We're not going to walk into their trap."

Viken curled his hands around the corners of his console. "You wish to retreat?"

"I wish to find another way across the sector." I scanned the warriors standing at their posts in leather battle kilts with battle axes hanging by their sides. Tails twitched and boots shuffled. "This is the most advanced horde in the galaxy, and this is the most well-trained crew. We need to get around this blockade. I trust my warriors can find a way."

Rolan threw his shoulders back. "You heard the Raas. Let's get to work."

Heads swiveled back and fingers tapped on screens. Rolan left his station to join me, turning to stand shoulder to shoulder and observe the urgent work of our warriors.

"You have a concern, *majak*?"

He didn't look away from the view screen. "Not a concern, Raas. A question."

"Ask it. You know I welcome your input and your counsel."

"What is our mission now, Raas? We joined the other hordes, intent on raiding one of the enemy battleships, but then we changed our plan to follow the transport. Once we took the human, we left the area quickly to put distance between ourselves and the admiral's search."

When he paused, I cut my eyes to him. "You want to know my strategy?"

"I would like to know our destination."

I couldn't suppress my grin. "That is a fair request. We need to get around the blockade so we can leave this sector and head to Zendaren."

His head snapped to me. "Zendaren? Home of one of our colonies?"

Even though I felt his gaze boring into me, I stared straight ahead. "While Viken and I were in the holo-ring, I was reminded that it had been too long since we returned. There are warriors who wish to hang up their battle axes and take a mate. There are sons who have not seen parents in longer than anyone can remember. I had promised a return before we'd intercepted the hail from my brother's horde. I do not want to go back on that just because we rescued the female."

"And this decision has nothing to do with the female?"

Now I did twist my head to his. "Why would it?"

"It is not related to what she conveyed about the admiral and his suspicions?"

My shoulders lowered. "Only in that I would like to reassure myself that all are safe, and there has been no security breach. Since we do not send communications to the colonies while we are away on our missions, there is no way to know if there has been any trouble."

"And you believe it is safe to visit?" Rolan asked. "With the admiral searching for them?"

Viken walked up and joined us, taking his position on my other side. We then stood three across, as we often did on the command deck, observing the warriors at work and monitoring the skies.

"Searching for what?" he asked.

"Raas wishes to set a course for Zendaren," Rolan said.

The effect on my battle chief was immediate. "The colonies?"

"It was our plan before we detoured to Carlogia Prime," I reminded him. "It is overdue."

"A trip to a pleasure planet is overdue," he mumbled.

Viken did not long for our return trips to the colonies, and would have much preferred to spend a few days drinking and whoring on Lissa.

"Is it wise to continue with that plan, Raas?" he asked. "If the empire has knowledge of the colonies' existence, shouldn't we avoid anything that might reveal their location?"

"The enemy cannot track us." I waved a hand at the motionless fleet in front of us. Not a ship had changed position, and not a weapon had been fired. "They cannot see us when we are right on top of them. How could they follow an unseen horde across two sectors and into an uncharted part of space?"

He nodded but scraped a hand through his sweaty hair. "We should increase our follow patrols during the journey."

"Agreed," I said. "I will count on you to make it happen."

"It is done, Raas." He clicked his heels. "I will go work on a patrol schedule for the trip, and draw up contingency battle plans."

He took long strides to his *oblek*, which was attached to one side of the command deck. Although the small, dim chamber was intended for interrogation, Viken preferred its solace—and the comfort of the surrounding weapons on the walls—when he made his plans.

"I've calculated a route around the blockade," one of my pilots said as he turned toward me.

"Transmit it to the horde ships on the encrypted channel," I said. "Then plot the most secure and least predictable route to Zendaren."

The command deck went quiet for a beat, even as the consoles emitted their intermittent beeps. Journeys to our secret colonies were always accompanied by caution and shrouded in layers of anxiety.

"But I would not be averse to including a pleasure planet as a stop along the way," I added.

The weight of the room lifted, and a collective breath was released. A roar of approval rose up, led by my own *majak*, who pumped his fist in the air.

It was clear my warriors needed a release before undertaking a trip that would be fraught with import and thick with responsibility. Not to mention the fact that it was, at heart, a trip home to visit family. That did not always equate to relaxation.

"You are sure?" Rolan asked in a voice only we two could hear.

"About the pleasure planet or the colonies?"

He didn't answer me directly. "How will you explain the human to *him*?"

He meant my uncle, the Raas who preceded me and who had been my mentor and father figure—much more than my own long-dead father. He lived on Zendaren, and I could not go without visiting him. Not that I would ever miss a chance to visit with the Vandar who had taught me everything I knew and gifted me with a triumphant horde.

But Rolan was right. A non-Vandar had never been to our secret colonies, especially not one who had been an imperial bride. Her presence would require an explanation for my uncle who insisted that every move be taken in service to a long-term strategy.

"Do not worry." I put a hand on my *majak's* shoulder. "I am not taking a human to our colonies. I will be taking my mate—a Raisa."

"I hope the human understands what that means, Raas."

My pulse quickened as I thought of her. So did I.

CHAPTER 13

Rachael

"What's going on?"

Even though I asked the question out loud as I paced beside the fireplace, there was no one in the room to hear me. Still, it was comforting to hear a sound other than the artificial snap of the blue flames. Since the ship's engines had stopped, things had seemed too quiet.

Why had the engines stopped? There had been no sounds of battle, so that wasn't the reason, and I doubted the Vandar warbird had suddenly broken down.

I took another gulp of my wine. I'd given up trying to pace myself, since it was clear the Raas wasn't coming back anytime soon. I didn't need to worry about staying sober and behaving myself if there was no one to behave in front of. I doubted my mother would have agreed with my logic, but at this point I could have cared less what she thought.

"It's her fault I'm in this mess," I whispered to myself. "Her and my father. Screw them."

I slapped a hand over my mouth as soon as the words left my lips. I never would have dared utter such a disrespectful thought on Horl. Not even to myself.

But you're not on Horl. You're on a Vandar ship, because your parents sold you off to a disgusting Zagrath admiral and you ran like hell.

"Screw them," I said again, this time louder.

Seriously. What kind of parents sold their daughter off to marry a man who could be her grandfather? I shuddered and slugged down more wine.

I couldn't feel my lips anymore, and my fingers tingled, but I didn't care. The Vandar wine helped keep me from thinking too much about the Raas' deal.

The whole thing still seemed unreal. Had the gorgeous alien—a warlord of the infamous Vandar raiders—really asked me to be his mate? It was crazy, especially since I'd barely been on the ship for any time at all and hardly knew him, but what was even crazier was that I was seriously considering accepting.

I held up my nearly empty goblet. "And that was before I was drunk."

I giggled and hiccupped and put a few fingers over my lips. It didn't matter that I was a little tipsy. It wasn't like I needed to be demure or well-behaved anymore. I was no longer a prize for my parents to show off. Suddenly, I felt freer than I ever had.

I may have technically been locked in the Raas' quarters, but I didn't answer to anyone anymore. I slammed back the last of the wine and scanned the sparse room.

Too bad there wasn't much I could do with my freedom. The bed loomed large, with its imposing posters and heavy drapery swagged over the canopy, but I wasn't sleepy. My stomach fluttered at the idea of being in bed when the Raas returned. Would he want to sleep or would he…?

I jerked my gaze away. An attendant had removed all the plates of food from the long table, but I did spot the carafe of wine. Walking quickly to it—and holding my arms out for balance—I refilled my goblet and took a sip. That was better.

Why was I even entertaining the idea of becoming a mate to a Vandar warlord?

"Aside from the fact that he's gorgeous?" I whispered to myself before stifling a giggle.

Raas Toraan definitely stirred something in me, his primal energy provoking my own deeply buried urges. And his tail… I moaned as I thought about how the tip of his tail twitched and wondered if the furry part felt as silky as it looked.

I tossed back a gulp of wine. Aside from desiring him, why would I want to commit myself to someone I barely knew? I'd already done that once when I'd been promised sight unseen to the admiral, and that hadn't gone well at all. Now that I was finally free from my parents and the empire, was I really ready to give up my freedom and promise myself to another?

Taking long steps to the fireplace inset in the obsidian wall between the Raas' quarters and the Raisa suite, I peered into the blue flames. But did I really have another option? If I rejected the Raas, what would the Vandar do with me? They didn't keep females on their warbirds, especially ones who weren't Vandar and had no reason to be there.

For the moment, I held some leverage. I'd told Toraan about the admiral's hunt for the colonies, and that had seemed valuable to him. But once I told him everything I knew, he would have no reason to keep me. I'd seen enough of the Raas to know that he wasn't some mindless brute like the Zagrath wanted people to believe.

No, he was smart and shrewd, but also, I suspected, ruthless in the pursuit of his enemy. He kept me because I had crucial information and because he believed taking me as a mate would strike a blow to the admiral. If I did not agree to be his mate, what would he do with me?

I closed my eyes for a moment, trying to imagine living my life with a virtual stranger aboard a raider warbird. Could I do it? Could I accept a future surrounded by huge, tailed aliens always on the hunt for battle? If not, could I give up the possibility of a future with *him*? He was the only male who'd ever provoked such sensations in me. I might have little experience with males and none with love, but I knew myself enough to know that I wanted to know him more. And I definitely knew I did not want to go back to the admiral or my parents or be dropped off at some random outpost.

Resting a hand on the obsidian stone hearth that was surprisingly cool to the touch, I opened my eyes and saw that the room swayed slightly. I eyed my nearly empty wine goblet. Despite how it warmed my belly, I suspected Vandar wine wasn't helping me think.

The doors behind me swished open. I turned quickly, then braced a hand on the hearth again for balance and took a deep breath to steady myself.

"I'm glad you are awake." Raas Toraan approached me quickly, his expression stern.

Damn. He did not look happy. Was he upset I hadn't given him an answer yet?

"I thought of something else," I said, the words spilling from me. I hoped he didn't hear the slight slur in them.

He stopped in front of me and titled his head to one side. "Something else?"

"About the Zagrath." My voice sounded tight, so I exhaled to calm myself as I set my goblet down on a nearby end table. I also needed a beat to figure out what I was going to tell him. What else did I know?

He crossed his thick arms over his chest. "If it is to do with the blockade, you are too late."

I blinked up at him, trying to process his words as my mind whirred. "Blockade? It is for me?"

"We believe so. The admiral's transmission was specific, and the blockade seems to be an attempt to force our hand. Not that we have any intention of being bullied by the empire."

"So, what are you going to do?"

"What we always do. Out-maneuver them." His gaze held mine. "And anyone who tries to deceive us."

I didn't know anything about the blockade, but I could see the suspicion on his face as he glowered at me. "I'm sorry. I had no idea—"

"None?" He cut me off, narrowing his eyes until they were slits.

I shook my head vigorously, which was a mistake, as my vision started to swim. "How could I have known that, especially if they did it to find me?"

"Perhaps it was always part of the Zagrath plan?" He stepped closer, towering over me. "You did say the admiral spoke freely around you."

"Not about any blockade." I sucked in a breath and thought back to the old man droning on about tracking the Vandar. Even though I'd attempted to tune him out a lot, my memory did not allow me to forget anything. "He did mention tracking the Vandar using cargo intended to be stolen during raiding missions."

His hazel eyes held me. "Anything else you forgot to mention before?"

My mind searched for any tidbit I could share with him. It was clear he thought I'd held out on him. Instead of worrying about him taking me as a mate, I was now concerned he might consider me a traitor and put me out an airlock.

"A star chart," I finally said. "I remember that he had a star chart—an old-fashioned one on paper so it couldn't be hacked into, he said."

Toraan's eyebrows lifted in obvious curiosity. "What did this star chart show?"

"He was tracking Vandar movements. Every time one of your hordes raided an outpost or a ship, he marked it. The admiral claimed that there were patterns."

Toraan closed his eyes for a moment before growling low and opening them again. "Just what we need. A Zagrath who can predict our horde patterns."

A word bubbled up in my mind, one the admiral had muttered to himself darkly many times. "Does the word amoeba mean anything?"

The Raas froze, then his hand darted out and grabbed my arm roughly. "Where did you hear that?"

I gasped as he jerked me to him. "The admiral said it. That was what he was attempting to break. Something about an amoeba, but I didn't know what the word meant." I tried to shake off Toraan's hand, but his grip was too tight. "I thought he'd made it up. I thought he was old and delusional."

Toraan released me, scraping a hand through his hair. "*Tvek*. If the enemy deciphers our amoeba defense…" He glanced at me. "It could mean death for all of us, including you."

I wasn't sure exactly what *tvek* meant, but at that moment, I felt like saying it a few times.

CHAPTER 14

Toraan

"You are sure, Raas?" Rolan's hands gripped the edge of the desk in my strategy room as he sat against it.

"How would she know the word if she had not heard the admiral use it?"

Rolan and Viken both nodded, but their faces were grim. They knew what this meant, just as I did. The amoeba defense was a tightly held secret that was one of the reasons we'd been able to evade the empire for so long and win so many battles. Its seeming unpredictability—along with our invisibility shielding — had made it almost impossible to defend against a Vandar attack. But if they knew about it and were working on determining the pattern…?

"I do not understand how this could have reached Zagrath ears." Viken slammed his palm against the star chart and the clear surface rattled from the impact.

"Too much has reached the Zagrath lately," Rolan added.

I agreed, but I could not imagine how it was happening, either. Our hordes were tightly contained communities. We did not interact with other species, and even rarely with other hordes. We flew stealthily and attacked our enemy without warning.

"The only variable is the human females," Viken said. "Your brothers both took one onto their warbirds, as you have done."

I flinched from the implied rebuke, and for the first time in ages, felt the urge to rush to my brothers' defense. "You believe humans—females at that—are behind the empire's intelligence on us? From what I understand, both females were their captives."

Rolan lifted his hands up. "Do you have another possibility, Raas?"

The only other possible answer was a traitor within, and the concept was abhorrent to me, as I knew it would be to my fellow raiders. "None that makes sense."

Viken planted his feet wide and braced one hand on the hilt of his battle axe. "We should consider more seriously that the human we have on board is part of the enemy plan."

"Then why did she tell us of the Zagrath's intel and plans?" I pointed to the star chart I'd marked with new points and waved a piece of paper in the air. "Why did she draw the admiral's star chart for me?"

Rolan eyed the paper. "How did a female with no astrological training replicate a star chart for you?"

I'd wondered the same thing when Rachael had begun sketching on the paper I'd found for her. "She claims to have a memory that allows her to recall anything she sees."

Rolan's eyebrows shot skyward. "Then perhaps she should be on the command deck instead of locked in the Raisa suite."

Viken snorted a laugh, and I didn't tell either warrior that she was staying in my quarters now.

"The fact remains that she knows what no female from Horl ever could without having heard it from the empire. And, until now, we have never been aware of the enemy having knowledge of our amoeba defense." I pointed to the star chart. "And there is no denying that this is a record of our horde's movements over the past astro cycle."

Both raiders shifted uncomfortably before nodding their agreement.

"The accuracy of this chart does lend strength to the rest of her information," Rolan admitted. "We should take it seriously."

"We should postpone our trip to the pleasure planet," I said.

Viken tightened his grip on his weapon. "As much as I hate it—and I do hate it—I agree. I do not know how, but the enemy has knowledge of us they did not have before. We should be more wary and unpredictable. And our stops on pleasure planets have been noted on this star chart."

I sighed. "The crew will be upset."

"The crew will survive." Viken gave me a crooked grin. "And they have their hands."

Rolan's gaze rested on me. "You are not still considering taking the human as a mate, are you, Raas?"

My initial anger at Rachael had faded, as had my belief that she had lied to me. She'd seemed genuinely contrite that she hadn't told me earlier, and part of me wondered if she had any idea of the importance of the information she'd overheard. To her, it had been boring chatter by the admiral and even terms she didn't understand. She'd seemed truly shocked that it had been so crucial.

Although I no longer seethed with fury, the seed of doubt had been planted. Lila had deceived me, and the betrayal I'd felt had pierced me deeply. It was one of the reasons I held honesty at such a premium. Could I trust Rachael? And if I couldn't, how could I possibly take her as a mate. I'd initially thought I could take a mate as a strategic move in my long game against the empire, but was I being reckless? A Raisa who was part of an imperial plot would be my undoing.

"Raas?" my majak prodded.

I swiveled my head between my two most trusted warriors. "Do you believe the female is in league with the empire?"

Both Vandar considered my question, then Rolan shook his head.

"I do not either," Viken admitted. "I believe she is in as much danger from them as we are, especially if the admiral has any clue that she listened as well as she did."

"Just because she is not a spy does not mean you need to take her as your Raisa," Rolan said.

"No." I tipped my head back and stared up at the black ceiling—the ambient lighting glowing blue across its surface—thinking of the pretty female I'd left in my quarters and trying to convince myself that she was not Lila. "It does not."

I did not need to take her as a mate. There were other ways to strike a blow to the imperial admiral. Then why did I want nothing more than for the human to say yes to me? Why did the need to claim her make my body throb and my pulse race?

CHAPTER 15

Rachael

"*Tvek, tvek, tvek!*" I was right. The Vandar curse word did help, even if I wasn't sure exactly what it meant.

I stomped across the room again, even though I'd practically worn a path in the shiny floor since Toraan had left me. He'd looked angrier when he left than when he'd arrived, and he hadn't been thrilled with me then, either.

Why had I held back from telling him everything I'd known? Now he'd lost faith in me, and he would probably doubt everything I did from here on out. If there was a "here on out." I couldn't imagine that he'd still want me as a mate. Not if he thought I'd lied to him, or at least withheld information, which I could sense from his expression, was the same thing in his book.

Taking long strides to the table, I refilled my goblet and took a swig. I hadn't done it on purpose. Everything had happened so fast. He'd rushed off when I'd told him about the admiral searching for the secret colonies, and then I'd been distracted by his suggestion of being his mate and had forgotten the whole reason he'd taken me on board—because I'd promised to give him intel on the empire.

I'd meant to keep up my end of the bargain. I truly had, but fear had kept me from spilling everything all at once. Fear that what I knew wouldn't be enough. Fear that once the Vandar knew what I did they wouldn't keep me. Fear that Toraan would realize he'd made a mistake in asking me to be his mate and promising not to turn me back over to the empire.

Now, the Raas had even more reason not to want me. Despite my own hesitation about agreeing to be a virtual stranger's mate, tears pricked the backs of my eyes as I realized that it would probably never happen now. Not if he thought I'd been deceptive.

I drained the goblet and poured myself another glass, even though I knew I should slow down. The Vandar wine was dulling both the pain and regret. Blinking away my tears , I walked unsteadily toward the bathroom, ignoring the recurring sensation that the room was slanting to one side. I needed to stop rehashing the conversation in my mind. I needed to take my mind off Toraan and the mess I'd made of things—and I knew just what would do that.

Although the attached bathroom was constructed of the same obsidian stone as the rest of the Raas' quarters, tiny pinpoints of sapphire light embedded in the ceiling gave it a blue glow. A shiny counter ran along one wall, and next to it was an obelisk with squared off sides and lots of flat buttons. A round, tiered pool dominated the center of the room, with a wide ring of water at the base, and three smaller rings leading up to a top circular pool that might hold two people. As I walked around, I saw that each level had steps to the next but was divided by stone walls, and each level featured a different color of water.

I approached the tiered pools almost reverently, dipping my fingers into the water and almost moaning when I realized the crimson water was hot.

How long had it been since I'd had a proper bath? The sonic showers on the imperial ship had been efficient, but not enjoyable.

I eyed the water again then glanced back at the doorway. Why was I concerned about Toraan walking in on me bathing? He'd stormed out, and I doubted he was coming back anytime soon. Even if he did, it wasn't like he'd want to begin whatever claiming ritual would make our mating official. Not now.

A pang of regret made my eyes burn, but was quickly replaced by a flutter of nerves. Even though I was sad the possibility of sex with the huge Vandar was most likely off the table, I was also relieved. Not that the idea of being with the Vandar didn't make my heart pound and heat pulse between my legs. It did, big-time, but that didn't mean I was a wham-bam-thank you-Rachael kind of girl.

I laughed at that thought, the sound echoing in the room.

"You need to relax," I told myself. "Everything is going to be fine."

I hoisted myself up on the stone wall of the pool and then swung my body over the side, pulling up my skirt, lowering my legs into the water, and letting out a breathy sigh.

Damn, that felt good.

I scissored my legs back and forth, mesmerized by the red of the water and how quickly the heat made the muscles in my shoulders unwind. I took a sip of wine then set my goblet on the stone ledge beside me.

What did it even mean to be a Raisa? Toraan had used that word and said it meant the mate of a Raas, but I wondered what would have been expected of me.

"Fuck him, obviously," I said to myself, the words giving me a small thrill. He was so huge, I could only imagine how large his cock would be. I gulped and moved my legs faster in the water, as some splashed over the sides. The stable boy I'd seduced hadn't been anywhere close to as big as the Raas, and I'd been sore after him.

I gave my head a small shake. "Better a huge cock than a shriveled one."

I bit back a giggle and a grimace, grateful that I would never have to see the admiral's old cock, which must have been as saggy and wrinkled as the rest of him.

My mind returned to the Raas. Even though I probably wouldn't be his Raisa now, I couldn't stop myself from thinking about it. He'd talked about mating marks that I would get. I touched a hand to my chest. It was strange to think of my brown skin with dark swirls across it, but not altogether unwelcome. I would have done anything that kept me out of the hands of the empire. Now, what would I do?

The warm water didn't seem so warm anymore as my legs had adapted to the heat, but I eyed the level higher. That water was orange, with bubbles popping at the surface, and I detected a spicy scent. I glanced down at my skirt and top. If I wanted to try out all the levels of the pool, I'd have to either take them off, or get them soaked.

I looked over my shoulder. I was still alone. As far as I knew, the Raas might not return for a while. If at all. The ship's engines hadn't started back up again, so whatever the issue was, it hadn't been solved. Not to mention the fact that he was most likely in counsel with his first mate about the information I'd finally given him.

I nibbled the corner of my lip. Then, before I could have second thoughts, I swung my legs back over the wall and quickly stripped off my clothes. I left them in a pile on the floor and quickly got back into the water, this time submerging myself in the heat up to my neck.

The shock of the water had sobered me up a little, but I didn't want to be sober. I wanted to forget the loss and fear and disgust I'd felt as I'd been handed over to the admiral and then escaped from him. And I needed to forget the frustration that I'd messed up the possibility of being with Raas Toraan.

I closed my eyes and sank into the water, my body floating on the surface and my ears submerged. I almost jerked back up when I heard music, but then I realized that it was playing underneath the water. The melody was soothing, and my anxiety melted away as I slowly let my body sink below entirely. For a moment, I was lulled by the sound and completely at peace.

Then a loud splash jerked me back to reality, and strong hands wrenched me out of the water. I gasped for breath as the Raas held my naked body to his.

CHAPTER 16

Toraan

At first I hadn't heard her when I'd entered my quarters, but a quick scan of the space—partially illuminated by the undulating, blue flames of the fire—had revealed that she wasn't sleeping or sitting at the table. The small splash from the bathing chamber had drawn me toward the room, even as my heartbeat had quickened.

Was she bathing? I hadn't explained the bathing pools to her, or which water held which healing property, but perhaps she had not been able to resist the temptation of the waters. The thought of the human naked in the water fired my blood and made my cock harden. I stripped off my armor and boots, discarding them—along with my battle axe—on the floor, then took long steps toward the bathing chamber.

Entering the space, my eyes adjusted to the blue lights embedded in the ceiling that gave it a starlight effect. My breath caught. Where was she? Moving quickly, I circled the tiered bathing pools and returned where I'd begun, seeing nothing. Then I spotted movement on the surface and a fingertip fluttering out of the crimson water.

She was submerged. I didn't pause to wonder why she might be beneath the water or hesitate to jump in, even though I still wore my battle kilt. I plunged my arms under the hot water and jerked her body to the surface, holding her to me as water streamed from her face and she spluttered and blinked.

"What the hell are you doing?" She pressed her hand to my chest, attempting to push herself away from me.

"Saving you." Her round breasts were against my chest, her skin warm and soft. I had one hand on the small of her back and my arm possessively wrapped around her shoulders.

She pushed firmly away from me, and I released my grip, immediately missing the feel of her. My gaze went to her breasts—the dark peaks tight—and my cock ached with desire. Even spluttering and angry, she was the most beautiful female I'd ever seen.

Smoothing her hair off her forehead, her previously bouncy, black curls now hung straight and wet. "Saving me?" She shook her head, then seemed to realize her breasts were exposed above the water and slapped her arm across them. "From what? Is the ship under attack? Are there intruders on board?"

I stared down at her, trying to keep my eyes from the soft mounds she attempted to hide. "No. I thought you were..." What had I thought? That she was drowning in water that did not reach above her chest? That she'd been trying to kill herself?

Before I could finish my explanation, or determine what exactly it was, she glanced down at me. "Are you still in your skirt?"

I followed her gaze to the leather that was now wet and heavy around my waist. "It is not a skirt. It is a Vandar battle kilt."

"Okay, but why are you wearing it in the bath?"

A flash of irritation made me growl. "I thought you were in some kind of distress. I was trying to save you."

Her gaze lowered. "I thought you never wanted to see me again the way you ran out earlier."

I thought back to my stormy exit. "I needed to share what you told me with my command officers. I am sorry if I led you to believe…"

"That you hated my guts and were regretting ever asking me to be your mate," she finished for me, her gaze darting to mine before dropping again.

"I never hated you. I was upset to learn that the enemy knows as much as they do, and I reacted strongly."

She gave a single nod but did not look up. "I should have told you sooner. I don't know why I didn't. It's all been such a whirlwind and then you mentioned being your mate, and I didn't know what to think about that. I mean, we hardly know each other and that's a big step, and then I guess I forgot that I'd promised to tell you everything I knew. Then you ran in talking about the blockade, and I remembered things. I never meant to keep secrets from—"

I put a finger to her lips to stop the nervous chatter spilling from her like water from a Vilidian geyser. "I understand."

Finally, she peered up at me. "You do?"

"I forget that all this is new to you, and you are still recovering from your escape from the empire. I should not have added my idea to be mates on top of everything."

"Oh." She bit her lower lip. "Do you want to take it back? I wouldn't blame you if you did."

Even though I'd considered it, looking down at her amber eyes framed with long lashes banished all thoughts of that from my mind. In that moment, I did want her to be my mate—and I knew deep down that strategy had little to do with it anymore. "I did not say I wanted to take it back, but you have also not given me your answer."

She furrowed her brow. "So, you still want to take me as a mate? You don't have to. I've told you everything I remember, and if I think of anything else, I'll tell you anyway. Just please don't return me to the admiral."

Even with her hair wet and water dripping down her face, she was beautiful. My heart squeezed as she peered up at me. "I promised you sanctuary, and I have no intention of going back on my promise. Just as I have no intention of taking back my request that you be my mate."

A smile teased the corner of her mouth. "In that case, yes."

"Yes?" Was she saying what I thought she was?

"I've decided I'll be your mate."

Warmth bloomed in my chest, taking me by surprise. "I am glad."

Rachael eyed me and my soaking wet kilt. "Are you sure this isn't one of your moves?"

"My moves? I do not understand."

Her tentative smile widened. "Saving the damsel in distress isn't part of the Vandar seduction playbook?"

I did not know what the female was talking about, but I did know that I was soaking wet in my battle kilt and still standing in the bathing pool. "The Vandar do not have a seduction playbook. We do not need one."

She gave me a look that told me she didn't believe me.

I hoisted myself over the stone ledge and landed on the floor, droplets splattering around me. "If you are fine, I will leave you to your bathing."

Rachael dipped below the surface of the water until only her shoulders were above. "You don't *have* to leave." She moved her arms out in front of her, her hands cutting through the water as if she was swimming. "You could join me."

Drops of water plopped steadily on the shiny floor beneath me as I stood watching her. Her pupils were wide, and she licked her lips as she eyed me. Was she suggesting what I thought she was? If so, she was embracing being my mate even more readily than I'd expected her to.

I loosened my belt and let it fall to the floor. Her eyes tracked my movements, her pupils widening as she stared at the bulge beneath my kilt.

"I wasn't sure when the agreement officially started. I mean, I didn't know when you wanted to…I assume to get mating marks we're supposed to…"

Her nervous patter of words was a reminder that she was younger than me, and no doubt much less experienced. If she'd been saved to be a bride for a Zagrath admiral, it was possible she was untouched. That thought made my own stomach flutter. The last thing I wanted to do was hurt her, even though I ached to claim her.

My gaze shifted to the goblet on the side of the pools and back to her flushed cheeks. "You've been drinking."

She twitched one shoulder up. "A little. Just while I was waiting for you. You were gone a long time, and I was worried."

"I would not take advantage of a female who has been drinking Vandar wine."

Her eyes narrowed. "Take advantage? You think I'm too drunk to know what I'm doing?"

I did not know her well enough to know how much wine she could tolerate, but Vandar wine was powerful, and she was slight. "I think we should wait until you have gotten some rest. You have had a long day."

She stood up fully in the water, smacking her palm against the surface. "You think I'm some kind a child who doesn't know her own mind, don't you?"

I wanted to tell her that I didn't, but my mouth had gone dry as she pulled herself over the stone ledge and swung her legs down to the floor. Water streamed down her naked body as she stood in front of me, her hands on her flared hips. I might have been terrified of the flash in her eyes if I hadn't been mesmerized by the sight of her perfect curves.

"I may not have traveled halfway across the galaxy like you, but I'm not a child who can be told what she needs." She closed the distance between us and dipped her hand beneath the sopping wet leather of my kilt, wrapping her warm hand around my cock before I knew what was happening. "I know exactly what I want, Toraan."

My cock was as hard as it had ever been in my life as her small fingers moved up and down.

Tvekking hell! The female had me by the cock. So much for not taking advantage of *her*.

CHAPTER 17

Rachael

I wasn't sure why I'd decided to grab his cock, but once I did, I couldn't exactly back down—even though my hand wouldn't close all the way around the huge thing, and it was even longer than I'd expected.

Not your best move, Rachael. You wanted to show him that you're a grown woman. Now what?

This wasn't the same thing as seducing the stable boy. Toraan was a Raas of the Vandar and about twice the size of the boy I'd sweet-talked into taking my virginity in the hay loft. He was the warlord of a violent horde of aliens. Not to mention, he had a tail and carried an axe.

My heart beat fast as I stared up at him. He'd barely flinched since I'd grabbed him, his muscles taut and only the very tip of his tail quivering. He was clearly trying to control himself, as he clenched his hands by his sides, and his molten gaze bored into me.

Even though we'd just made a deal to become mates, I didn't know him, and he didn't know me. But for some reason, I desperately wanted to prove myself to him—to prove I wasn't as clueless or inexperienced as he probably thought I was.

Dropping my gaze, I swallowed hard as the blood thundered in my ears. Dropping my gaze, I found the buckle to his kilt and worked it with one hand, the other still firmly gripping his cock. When I got it unfastened, I moved my hand, and the wet leather fell to the floor.

"You should not," he said, his voice husky and low.

My eyes were riveted to the sight of his cock—thick, and etched with dark swirling marks as it jutted out from his body. I hadn't known the Vandar mating marks were also on their cocks. I ran my fingers over the curling lines, curiosity overpowering my nerves. "Why not? I thought this was what you wanted. Isn't this what mates are supposed to do?"

Although my words sounded confident, my pulse was going like a trip wire. Even the Vandar wine, which had made me feel sexy and powerful when I was in the bathing pools, was only a memory. Touching him had cleared the fog from my head, although heat pulsed between my legs as I stroked him.

He reached a hand down and clamped it over mine, stopping my fingers from feathering over the surprisingly velvety skin of his shaft. "Not when you are drunk on wine and not thinking straight."

I tried to tug my hand from his grip. "Who says I'm drunk?"

He did not release my hand. "You are slurring your words."

Shit. So much for sounding sophisticated and sultry. I must have sounded ridiculous. The back of my eyes burned as humiliation washed over me. Instead of making myself look worldly, I must have seemed even more like a child to him. A child who couldn't hold her liquor.

"Fine. If that's what you want." My cheeks burned as I jerked my hand back harder, and he released me. I attempted to walk out of the bathroom with as much dignity as I could, but when I reached the bedroom, it struck me that my clothes were behind me on the floor.

I stifled a groan. No way was I going back for them. I stomped to the bed and pulled back the dark, silky sheets. Even though I was dripping water, I got in bed and tugged the sheets up over my shoulders, turning away from the bathroom door.

Had Toraan actually turned me down? I fumed as I lay in bed. Who cares if I drank a little wine? Anyone would need a few drinks to handle what he had between his legs. My pulse fluttered just thinking about it, and imagining what it would be like inside me. The stable boy had been fun, but he hadn't prepared me for *that*.

There were no sounds behind me—not the sounds of the Raas storming out or getting dressed or even splashing in the pools. I lay in the dark room and sleep began to overtake me. As much as I did not want to admit that I was tired, my eyes sagged with exhaustion and a yawn escaped my lips.

Then the bed shifted next to me as Toraan's heavy body got in on the opposite side. Even though the bed was large, he was so much heavier than me that the pillowy surface sank under his weight, and I rolled toward him. I put my hands out, keeping my body from bumping into his, and my fingers touched bare flesh. The Vandar was completely naked.

"You aren't wearing anything," I said.

"Neither are you."

He had a point. I'd never actually slept naked. On Horl, I'd had a collection of prim nightgowns, and my mother had dutifully packed a collection of new ones when she'd sent me off to marry the admiral. They had long sleeves and high necklines, and she'd instructed me to keep them on and let my husband move them aside as needed. "I don't have anything to wear to sleep."

"Vandar do not wear clothes when we sleep."

"Oh." The thought of sleeping naked beside the warlord every night sent a thrill through me. "Even the females?"

"Even the females." His voice held a hint of amusement. "Does it bother you to be unclothed? Would you feel safer if you slept in the Raisa's chamber?"

I glanced at the doorway on the other side of the room, shaking my head as I thought of the sadness that hung over that bedroom like a shroud. "No way."

He cocked his head at me. "It is that bad? I have always thought it was an appropriate sleeping chamber."

"I'd rather sleep naked than sleep in there." I said, even though sleeping without clothes would take some getting used to. There was a lot on the alien ship that did not feel natural. I would have to adapt to the Vandar traditions if I was to be the Raas' mate. "Is it normal for Vandar males and females to have separate bedrooms?"

"No, but the Raisa it was built for was delicate and needed a great deal of sleep. My uncle, who preceded me as Raas, wanted to keep her close to him but he was known for his own restless sleep."

"I guess that makes sense, but it's also a little sad."

The Raas looked away from the doorway. "It does not matter. It was never used, and I have no intention of taking a mate and sending her to sleep alone." He met my eyes. "Is it customary on your planet for mates to sleep apart?"

I thought about my own parents and their separate bed chambers. "Even if it was, I wouldn't want to."

"No?"

I shook my head. "I want to please you, so you won't send me away."

He was quiet for a moment, then he shifted to face me in the dark. "I will never send you away."

"You don't know me. What if you discover that I snore or kick in my sleep? What if I steal the sheets? What if you decide you don't like me, and don't want to take me as your mate?"

"Do you snore?"

"I don't think so, but I've never shared a bed with anyone before."

"I have spent a good part of my life on a Vandar warbird surrounded by warriors. I was not always Raas. For ages, I served as an apprentice, which mean I slept in communal chambers. If I can sleep through the sounds of dozens of warriors snoring and grunting and pleasuring themselves, I can withstand the sounds of a tiny, human female." He reached out and stroked a finger down my cheek. "Are you afraid I will snore?"

I'd never thought of that. "Do you snore?"

This time he let out a throaty chuckle. "No."

"That still doesn't solve the problem of you not knowing me," I said. "How can you be sure you want me? I know you're doing this to strike a blow to the empire, but taking me as your mate means you have to live with me. According to my mother, I'm too independent."

"I like independent," he said. "I like that you ran from the empire. I like that you are unafraid. You will be a good mate to a Vandar."

"I'm not unafraid," I confessed.

"Are you afraid of me?"

"Not really. But you are bigger than any other male I've ever met. By a lot."

"That did not stop you from grabbing my cock."

My face heated, and I was glad he couldn't see it in the dark. "I was trying to behave like I thought a Vandar female would, and I wanted to please you."

"You do not need to worry about pleasing me." He cupped my chin in his hand. "There will be time for that when you are rested, and have not had an entire flagon of wine for yourself. Now, you should sleep."

The faint light from the fire outlined his face in the dark. Before I'd thought the shadows made him appear fierce. Now I wanted to touch the sharp lines of his face and to feel his skin. I put my hand on his cheek and leaned in, kissing him lightly on the lips. "Good night, Raas."

Instead of replying, he pulled my head to his, deepening the kiss. His lips were strong but also soft, and pleasure jolted through me as they moved against mine. When he pulled away, he dragged the pad of his thumb across my lips. "Good night, Raisa."

He rolled onto his back, leaving me breathing hard and more awake and aroused than I wished to be. I blew out a breath, feeling the slickness between my thighs. It was going to be a long night.

CHAPTER 18

Toraan

When I woke it was still dark. I had the lights in my quarters set to illuminate at a set time each cycle, but I could tell that it was long from the time I needed to rouse. For a moment, I wondered why I was awake, then I heard the breathy sounds next to me.

I stilled even more so I could be sure I was hearing what I thought I was. Although the room was dark—even the blue flames of the fire were low—it was clear that Rachael was moving next to me. Not a lot, but enough to explain the uneven breaths and the quiet jerks beneath the sheet.

At first, I was shocked that she was pleasuring herself while I slept. Then I reminded myself that I'd been the one to insist we go to sleep and then had kissed her intensely enough that my own arousal had kept me awake longer than I would have liked.

Then I thought about the pretty female touching herself, and any shock evaporated as my cock hardened.

I wanted to be absolutely motionless so I could enjoy the sounds of the female wriggling and panting, but my cock had another idea, tenting the sheet as it rose.

Rachael stopped. "Are you awake?"

"Yes, but you don't have to stop."

"Shit. You weren't supposed to wake up. I was trying to be quiet about it, since you thought I was too drunk on Vandar wine to do anything." Her voice got louder as she talked, and it ended up as almost a shriek.

"Are you angry with me?"

She exhaled loudly. "No."

"Would you like me to help?"

She head snapped over to me. "Help?"

Without saying another word, I tore back the sheets so I could see her. The points of her breasts were rock-hard, and her legs were slightly splayed. I rolled over so that I hovered above her, bracing my arms on either side of her.

"I thought you said you didn't want to…"

I shook my head. "I never said I didn't want to. I said I *should* not since you were under the influence of very strong Vandar wine."

"So, what changed?"

"Nothing." I leaned close and inhaled deeply at her neck. "I do not need to fuck you to give you pleasure."

Her body quivered as I moved my lips from her throat down to her chest, brushing them softly over her tight peaks, and then kissing my way down her stomach. When I reached her sex, I breathed deeply again, inhaling the intoxicating scent of her arousal. "Open your legs for me."

She didn't hesitate, spreading her legs for me so I could settle myself between them. I dragged a finger between her smooth folds, a low rumble escaping my throat. "You're soaked."

"Well, you got me kind of worked up."

"I did?" I looked up across the curves of her body, silhouetted in the dark. Even without much light, I could see her gaze locked on mine.

"With that kiss," she whispered. "No one has ever kissed me like that."

A strange sensation of pride and possessiveness stormed through me. I liked that no male had kissed her like I had. I met her gaze and held it. "You understand what it means to be mine? You know that no one will ever touch you again but me? Once you are claimed by a Raas, it is for life."

Her words were soft. "I understand."

I turned my attention back to her sex, dragging my tongue through her folds and flattening it over the bundle of nerves that was already slick and engorged. She arched her back, moaning and digging her fingernails into my shoulders.

I continued to lick her as I moved my tail up to caress her breasts, flicking the furry tip over them. Since the tip of my tail was the most sensitive part, the sensation of her pebbled flesh sent ripples of pleasure through me. I growled as I thought about all the other places I wanted to put my tail. More moaning and more fingernails in my flesh as she gyrated her hips.

These were not the sounds and movements I'd heard when I'd woken. These were more—more breathless, more desperate. She was letting herself go as she moved beneath me, her body jerking as I sucked her nub.

"Toraan," she gasped, wrapping her legs around my shoulders.

"Mmhmm." My humming response vibrated against her flesh and she bucked up, screaming out as she moved her hands from my shoulders to my head, tangling her fingers in my hair and holding me to her as she shook.

When she finally flopped back, she heaved in a breath. "I didn't know… I've never…You know way more than the horse master's assistant."

I lifted my head. "The horse master's assistant?"

She slapped a hand across her mouth. "I shouldn't have said that, especially after you just…"

"You do not have to hide your past from me," I said, shifting myself up so that my head rested on her stomach. "The horse master's assistant was one of your lovers?"

"One of?" She spluttered out a laugh. "Try the only one. My parents went to a lot of trouble to keep me pure so I could be an even more valuable prize for some imperial big-wig."

"You have only ever been with one male?"

She nodded. "I was supposed to save myself for the admiral, but I couldn't stand the thought of some old guy I didn't even know being my first, so I seduced the horse master's assistant out in our stable."

I should have been jealous that my mate had been with another, but instead I admired her rebellion. The thought of her taking charge of her own pleasure, much as she'd done tonight, only fueled my desire to claim her. The human was no timid creature who would shrink from life on a Vandar warbird or from the desires of a Vandar Raas.

"Did you like fucking this horse master's assistant?" I asked.

She hesitated. "It felt good after a while, but he didn't do anything to me like what you just did."

"No?"

She shook her head. "I don't think he'd been with many females. Not as many as you've probably been with."

I could sense the question in her words. If she was going to be my mate, she deserved to know about me. "It is common for Vandar raiders to visit pleasure planets for release."

"Pleasure planets?" She sat up on her elbows. "I've never heard of that."

I cocked an eyebrow at her. "You were sheltered. There are pleasure planets dotted across the galaxy where males and females can go to drink and whore and enjoy themselves with specially trained pleasurers."

"You pay for them?"

"Of course," I said, laughing. "More for some than for others, and more for certain fetishes."

She tilted her head at me. "Do you have any fetishes?"

"Nothing that is unusual for a Vandar," I told her.

I would wait to show her what I liked to do with my tail. But only when she was ready.

"Do you?" I asked.

She giggled and sank back onto the bed. "If loving whatever you just did to me is a fetish, then I've got that one."

CHAPTER 19

Rachael

The Raas was gone when I woke the next morning, as were his clothes and armor. I sat up and rubbed my head, wishing it didn't throb so badly.

"He was right about Vandar wine." Even though I whispered the words, I flinched from the sound of my own voice.

I'm never drinking again, I thought, wondering if the Vandar stocked any remedies for head pain. At least the room was still dimly lit, even though recessed lighting in the ceiling gave the room a warm glow it hadn't had last night.

Pulling the sheet around myself, I shivered as I padded to the bathroom. No flames crackled in the fireplace inset in the wall, which made the glossy black walls and floors seem even colder.

The clothes I'd thoughtlessly discarded were neatly folded and stacked on the long counter. I eyed the bathing pools, steam rising up from the largest ring on the bottom and bubbles breaking the surface of the orange water one level higher. The heat was appealing, but I wasn't in the mood for a soak. Not when it made me think about Toraan, half-naked and dripping wet.

My heart fluttered in my chest, and I groaned, touching my pounding temples. Even getting turned on made my head ache.

You can do this, Rachael. You just need to get dressed and get something to eat and try not to think about what actually happened last night.

Heat rushed south at the memory of the Raas' dark head buried between my thighs and the way my body had responded. If I'd had any plan to act coy or shy with him, that was officially shot to hell. My cheeks flamed as I remembered him waking and catching me pleasuring myself.

"That was not supposed to happen," I muttered to myself.

I'd never planned to take matters into my own hands. Then, again, I'd never suspected that the Vandar would refuse to fuck me just because I'd been drinking. Hadn't he been the one to suggest we be mates as part of his plan to keep me from Zagrath hands and hit the admiral where it hurt most? And hadn't I agreed with him, knowing fully well what it meant?

What I'd been expecting was a rough alien who was used to violence and would take what he wanted from me no matter what. I'd been braced for it. But he'd been nothing like what I expected, although I was not complaining about what he could do with his tongue.

My cheeks burned even hotter, and I shook my head. "Get it together, girl. He's still a Vandar, and he still plans to fuck you until you get his mating marks. It's a deal that benefits both of us, plain and simple."

Thinking of it that way made it easier for me to lose the sheet and pull on the clothes I'd been wearing the day before. I didn't mind the skirt that Toraan had called a kilt, but part of me felt funny to be showing so much leg after a lifetime spent wearing long dresses that pooled around my ankles and cuffed at my wrists. At least I wasn't in that absurd wedding dress. I hoped they'd put *that* thing out an air lock.

I glanced in the one of the round mirrors embedded into the stone wall above the counter. My hair had curled as it had dried in my sleep, dark ringlets now framing my face and bits of hair frizzing at my temples. I tried to loosen the curls with my fingers, but it didn't do much. I made a mental note to ask for a comb. I sighed as I finger-styled my hair. Or a hat.

A noise from the other room made me freeze. Had Toraan returned? I gave a final glance at my reflection and poked my head out of the doorway.

It wasn't Toraan. Another Vandar was entering the room with a large tray on his shoulder. He wasn't as big or as muscular as most of the other raiders I'd seen. Like the one who'd delivered the meal the day before, this one looked more like a boy. Even the tip of his tail was not as furry.

"Hello?" I said as I walked out.

The boy faltered slightly but managed to lower the tray to the table.

"Sorry." I walked over to him. "I didn't mean to startle you."

The boy glanced at me, his face flushing before he returned his gaze to the tray and the domed plates he was unloading. "The Raas said you would be sleeping."

"I was." I breathed in the savory aroma of the food, and my stomach lurched. I stepped back from the table and pressed my fingertips to my lips.

The boy swiveled his head to look at me, then he held out a goblet. "The Raas also said you'd need this."

I took the goblet and eyed the murky, green contents. "What is it?"

The boy's gaze dropped again. "A restorative. The Raas said humans are not used to Vandar wine."

So, it was no secret on the ship that I couldn't handle my wine? I frowned. I wasn't giving humans the best name so far.

I took a tentative sip of the concoction, cringing at the strange taste but forcing myself to swallow it. Pinching my nose, I downed the remains of the drink, squeezing my eyes shut and shuddering.

When I opened my eyes, the boy was staring at me.

"I've never seen someone drink it all at once."

I shot him a look. "You could have told me it that before."

He shrugged. "It's probably better for you that way." He gave me a quick up and down. "And you must be tougher than you look."

"Thanks." I handed him the empty goblet. I could see that he wore no battle axe on his belt like the other raiders I'd seen, only a blade tucked in his waistband. "Who are you? You're not a raider."

He straightened his shoulders. "I'm an apprentice raider."

That explained his age and his eagerness. "You're in training?"

He nodded, and his tail swished behind him. "All Vandar apprentice before they become raiders."

"So, you leave your families and live on a ship with all Vandar males?" I asked. "For how long?"

"As many standard rotations as it takes to prepare us to be the toughest, most ruthless warriors in the galaxy." His voice brimmed with pride.

"Even the warlords?" It was difficult to imagine Toraan—huge and serious and menacing—ever being as young and eager as this boy.

"Oh, yes. Raas Toraan served under his uncle for a long time. Raas Maassen was a great leader, who built our horde to be the largest in the Vandar empire."

I'd never seen a Vandar horde. It was a tricky proposition, since the ships flew invisibly. But I knew that they traveled in large groups of warbirds like a swarm. I'd heard the whispers, even on a planet as remote as Horl. The Vandar hordes appeared out of the blackness of space like wraiths, surrounding vessels and signaling their impending doom.

"Did Toraan inherit the horde when his uncle died?"

The apprentice's brow furrowed. "Raas Maassen is not dead. He is alive and well on Zendaren." He grinned at me. "I am sure you will be presented to him when we arrive."

"Presented?"

"Raas Toraan will have to present his mate to his uncle. I don't know if they'll insist on a ceremony there or not. I've never heard of a ceremony with a Raas and a human." The apprentice moved the domed plates around on the table and tucked the tray under his arm, then seemed to notice me gaping at him.

"You know about the… I mean, you know I'm…?"

"The Raas' mate?" He finished my sentence for me with a look that told me everybody on board knew. "Of course."

Okay. I wasn't sure how the Raas had explained it to his crew, but the apprentice didn't seem shocked. "Did you say something about arriving on…?"

"Zendaren—the Vandar colony."

My stomach, which had been feeling better, tightened. "We're going to the secret Vandar colonies?"

"One of them, although they're all pretty close."

We were on our way to the Vandar colonies Admiral Kurmog was determined to find and destroy? I wasn't sure if I should be more terrified of that, of being presented to the old Raas as Toraan's mate, or of a ceremony that might or might not take place.

As my mother would have said, I was out of the frying pan and into the flames.

CHAPTER 20

Toraan

"How many more do we need?" Rolan leaned his hand on the wall, as our chief engineer squatted over a power conduit near our engine.

The engineering section of the ship—located in the belly of the vessel—was illuminated with incandescent purple lighting that pulsed as the engine hummed. The rumbling was louder here, as the enormous cylindrical engine spun in the middle of the room surrounded by a vibrating, energy containment field. Although I knew the basics of engineering and how my warbird worked, I rarely thought about the complex systems that provided my horde ships with incredible speed and invisibility shielding.

"For a journey of this duration?" The raider swept a hand through his shaggy, black hair. "If we want to maintain invisibility, at least five more coils, and ten crystalline filters."

I grunted as Rolan added the supplies to our ever-growing list. We'd been doing a tour of the ship since the dawn of first watch, and it was clear that a supply run would be in order before we could make it to Zendaren. Crossing from our sector to Carlogia Prime had drained much of our reserves, and it had been a considerable amount of time since we'd carried out a successful raid that had produced any useful cargo.

I inclined my head at my chief engineer. "It is done."

He stood and snapped his heels together. "Thank you, Raas."

"We don't need to visit the food stores," Rolan said, as we turned to leave the enclosed section of the ship. "All we got from the last imperial ship we boarded was food."

"Unless we all grow weary of Gendarian spore bread."

My *majak* made a face, and glanced at the tablet in his hands. "I will add meat to our list."

"Anything but slug steaks," I told him.

"Agreed." He tapped at his screen without looking up at me as we made our way along the suspended iron walkway. "Do you require any special supplies?"

"Special supplies?" I paused as a pair of raiders passed us, clicking their heels without breaking stride. "Why would I require special supplies?"

He lifted his gaze to me. "I do not know if the human requires anything, or if you need anything in particular to best carry out your…mission."

I folded my thick arms across my chest. "I am not courting the female. This is a strategy against the empire."

"Of course, Raas." He took a breath as if strengthening himself. "But she is a female. Do you not want to perhaps acquire some Palaxian wine?"

I choked back a laugh. Rachael had been tipsy enough on Vandar wine. I could hardly imagine serving her Palaxian wine that was intended to cause arousal. I flashed back to the sounds of her pleasuring herself and then to the taste of her sweet juices on my tongue.

"Raas?"

I jerked my head up as Rolan eyed me curiously. Had I growled out loud, or was that only in my mind? Either way, I cleared my throat. "No Palaxian wine. I actually requested that wine *not* be taken to my quarters today."

My *majak's* eyebrows lifted. "Does she not drink?"

"Oh, she drinks, which is why I requested no wine. I would prefer that she not be drunk when I come back to my quarters. Last night she drank an entire flagon of Vandar wine."

"Curious." Rolan tapped a finger to his tablet. "She is so small. It is hard to image her finishing that much wine by herself. She looked almost like a girl when she disembarked from the imperial transport."

"She is no girl," I barked, thinking of her legs circling my shoulders and her body bucking against me. "I would never claim a female who is not of age."

"I didn't mean to say— "

I clapped a hand on my *majak's* arm to stop his spluttered explanation. "I know you didn't." I huffed out a breath and resumed walking. "It is this journey that is making me on edge. It has been a long time since we have returned to Zendaren."

My pace had increased as I'd been talking, and by the time we reached the cargo bay, I was practically jogging. I pressed my hand to a side panel, and the tall, double doors swept open. The steel crates that usually packed the expansive space had dwindled—a stark reminder that our supply run would be none too soon.

"It has been, but you have never been concerned about returning to the colonies."

"This is different."

"Because of the imperial threat, or because you will be bringing a mate?"

"The threat," I lied. In truth, no Vandar had ever brought a human to the colonies, and certainly not a mate he intended to make his Raisa. I knew as well as anyone that it was not done.

We did not speak as we entered the cargo bay, the ambient lights flickering overhead.

"You do not have to take the female as your mate, Raas." My *majak's* voice was low and furtive, as we walked among the crates stacked in even rows. "We can always claim her as property of the Vandar, and that will be that. Is that not what your brother, Raas Kratos, did with his human?"

"The one who is now his Raisa?"

Rolan tilted his head at me with a wry smile. "That is a good point, Raas."

I gave a brusque shake of my head. "My brother did not take his female to protect her from the empire. He took her to punish her for flying into Vandar space. There was no powerful, imperial admiral hunting her down. I am doing this because this female means something to the empire and to one of its most important leaders. This is a blow to an empire that thinks they can take any planet they want and enslave alien populations for their own benefit. They have been claiming other species' property for millennia—including our own home world. Now, we are taking something of value to them, and claiming it as ours forever."

"The risk is not too great?"

"To the female?" I asked, then shook my head. "Not with the firepower of a Vandar horde between her and the empire."

"To you."

I pivoted slowly to face him. "You believe I am putting myself in greater danger than I already am as a Raas of the Vandar?"

"You do not fear forming an attachment?" He answered my question with one of his own. One we both understand without him saying more. Rolan knew very well about Lila. He had been the first to hear of her betrayal when we'd arrived back on Zendaren, and the one to tell me. His face had been just as twisted with concern then as it was now, and I was transported to that moment when my world had cratered. Anger and hurt rushed in as fresh as it had been the moment he'd relayed the news.

I pushed the ache aside and turned away from him. "This is about revenge, not love."

"Against Lila?"

The name of my former love spoken aloud was like a blow, but I shook it off. "Against the empire."

"If you are sure, Raas," he said, "but you have not seen her since that time. Are you sure you should bring the human? You will not have formed mating marks. Your attachment will not be secure."

My heart thundered in my chest. Who was my *majak* to question my strategy against the empire or my intentions in visiting our colonies? If the human was fine with our agreement, why should he concern himself? It was a deal between us to protect her and to inflict pain on the admiral.

"I promise you it will be secure," I growled. My fingers twitched above the hilt of my battle axe until I steadied my breath. It was not Rolan who angered me—it was that he knew me so well and that he knew of my pain and humiliation.

Even though it was his job as my first officer and most trusted advisor, it was a painful part of my past. One I'd worked hard to forget. Serving as a Vandar Raas had kept me busy enough, and pleasurers had served as welcome distractions, but I'd hardened my heart to all else. It had been my plan to serve as Raas until I was struck down in battle, instead of leaving the horde to take a mate. Until Rachael had come on board. Not that taking her as a mate would mean leaving the horde. That was not part of the deal.

I told myself that it had been an easy sacrifice from one who had no intention of ever making a love match. In truth, taking a mate as part of a military strategy fueled both my desire to punish the empire, and my inexplicable need to protect Rachael. A need I could not confess to my *majak*, who might think it meant more.

I thought of the beautiful female, and my cock twitched. She was certainly arousing enough to keep me interested, although I had steeled myself to the possibility of anything more than a physical connection. Still, it would be no hardship to bed her—one of the steps that would ensure she took my mating marks.

"You are right about one thing," I told Rolan as I stalked out of the cargo bay without a backward glance. "I need to get to work on those mating marks."

CHAPTER 21

Rachael

I'd finished the breakfast the apprentice had set out for me, and had been pacing for a while. I was too jittery to sit and watch the fire, which the apprentice had activated for me, and even a soak in the tubs didn't appeal. At least the repulsive drink had cured my nausea, but I swore I'd never drink so much Vandar wine again in my life.

"Where are you?" I whispered, eying the door for a hundredth time.

The Raas wasn't seriously going to leave me alone all day every day, was he? There was nothing to do in his spartan quarters, except stare out the wide wall of glass as the ship sped through space. Occasionally, we'd pass a hunk of rock, but all in all, interstellar travel was extremely boring.

Having nothing to distract me meant I was alone with my thoughts, and that was the last thing I wanted. I did not want my mind to wander to my parents, or my home planet of Horl. By now, they would know that I'd escaped. Were they worried that their daughter was alone in space and possibly in danger, or were they more angry that I hadn't gone through with my wedding to the admiral? Knowing my parents and how they'd treated me like chattel to be auctioned off to the highest bidder, I honestly didn't know.

I walked to the glass overlooking space and put my hands to the cool surface. My home world was out there somewhere, even if it felt like my life there was a lifetime ago. My throat thickened, as I realized that I'd probably never see it again. Not if I kept up my end of the bargain with Raas Toraan.

A Vandar horde had no reason to go to Horl. It was a planet that had been loyal to the empire for longer than I'd been alive. Like everyone in the galaxy, we'd heard about the raider hordes, but never had one appeared in our skies.

No, agreeing to be the Raas' mate might keep me from the admiral, but it also ensured that I'd never again lay eyes on the rolling hills and cliffside towns that made Horl so prized by the empire. Unlike other planets, with rich stores of resources to be mined, Horl provided grain, produce, and renowned wine, so our verdant farmland was unspoiled.

I twisted my head to take in the sleek space that was dominated by polished black stone and hard surfaces. It was a far cry from the arched mansion I'd lived in, with light streaming in from wide windows, and gossamer curtains fluttering in the breeze.

"This is where you live now," I told myself, hoping the force of my words would staunch the tears that threatened to fall.

Had I made a mistake in agreeing to the Raas' deal so quickly? I'd been so eager to get away from the admiral that I hadn't thought things through, or considered what living with a Vandar horde meant. I hadn't known. All I'd been sure of was that it would be better than life in a loveless marriage with a disgusting old man.

I shivered at the memory of him. I had definitely been right to run from Admiral Kurmog. Even if my deal with the Raas was only military strategy for him and escape for me, he was a much more appealing bed mate. I didn't even care if he was using me, and I was using him. Our pact might not be about love, but that didn't mean I wouldn't enjoy every minute of being used by him to enrage the admiral.

The doors behind me slid open, and I whirled around, my cheeks warming as Raas Toraan entered. Why did I feel like he'd caught me doing something naughty again?

"You are up," he said, not pausing as he took long steps toward me.

"Did you think I'd still be sleeping?" I had no concept of time in a room with no timepieces and no suns to rise and fall, but I suspected he'd been up for a long time.

He reached me, coming so close I felt the need to back up, but the only thing behind me was the glass wall. "You were sleeping deeply when I left and snoring very loudly."

My mouth dropped open. "I was not!"

His mouth twitched, and his severe expression faded for a moment. "No, you were not."

I wanted to smack him, but he was looming over me, his gaze intense. I instantly decided not to complain about being left alone or ask him what was going to happen when we reached the Vandar colony. "Is everything okay?"

He inclined his head. "We were able to route ourselves around the imperial blockade and set a new course. The horde will need to stop for supplies and for recreation before we reach our destination, but neither stop will be long."

"How does a horde stop for recreation?" I asked, envisioning a massive fleet of ships docking on Horl and raiders flooding the seaside.

"The pleasure planets I mentioned last night." His gaze moved across my face, and he brushed a curl off my forehead. "I forget you have never left your planet before and that Horl is known for being quite . . . restrictive in its customs."

His judgment of my home world struck a nerve. "How do you know anything about it? Have you ever been there?"

"No." His deep voice did not match my raised one.

I put my hands on my hips. "Then you don't know what it's like, do you? It's actually a beautiful planet."

"Controlled by the empire."

I flinched at that. He was right, of course. Horl was under total Zagrath control—and it was probably more restrictive in every way than Vandar culture. One glance at his exposed skin, and I knew that.

"Fine. Horl is uptight compared to the Vandar, but it's not like we don't know how to enjoy ourselves. You've never lived until you've galloped across an open meadow on the back of a horse, as the two suns set over the horizon."

He rested a hand on my waist as if he was holding me to him. "And many of my raiders would argue that you have not lived until you have had a set of Felaris twins sucking your cock in tandem."

I drew in a quick breath. "Is that what you do on pleasure planets?"

"Not always what *I* do, but pleasure planets are for fulfilling your carnal desires."

I wasn't sure what to say to that. Carnal pleasures were definitely not something to be discussed on Horl or encouraged, especially for females. "And we're going to one of these pleasure planets?"

"My raiders need a release before we continue to the Vandar colonies. It has been a long time since they have done anything but fly and raid."

I wanted to ask him if he would be going down to the planet, but I also didn't feel like it was my place. It wasn't like we were together in a traditional way. Sure, I was going to be his mate, but only because it served both of our purposes, not because we were passionately in love. Still, I disliked the idea of him with anyone else, especially twins.

"I will not be joining my raiders at the pleasure houses." It was as if he'd read my mind.

I tipped my head back to meet his eyes. "Really? Does the Raas not leave his ship or something?"

"No. I typically avail myself of the pleasurers." He lifted a hand to cup my face. "But this time, I have other things to do."

My mouth went dry. "What kind of things?"

His eyes burned into me as he dragged a thumb across my jaw. "Did you think I forgot last night, or what you wanted from me?"

My memories were a bit fuzzy, although I remembered every moment of his head buried between my legs. "No, but— "

"I also have not forgotten our deal, have you?"

I shook my head, my pulse fluttering madly. "No, Raas."

He moved his hand from my jaw, tracing one fingertip down my neck to my chest and sliding it over my exposed cleavage. "If I'm going to put mating marks on this perfect skin, I will need to spend most of my time in bed with you."

I tried to speak, but only a strangled sound emerged from my lips.

Lowering his head, he brushed his lips across mine. "Starting now."

Then he flattened me against the wall, and crushed his mouth to mine.

CHAPTER 22

Toraan

I parted her lips with my tongue, moaning as I savored the sweetness of her. My body was hard against hers, even as she arched into me.

Taking one wrist in my hand, I lifted her arm over her head and pinned it to the glass. She tried to pull it away, but I held tight. Then I took her other hand and pinned it to the small of her back, never breaking our kiss. I used my tail to stroke up the inside of her thigh as her moaning grew louder.

When I tore my mouth from hers, her eyes were dazed and her chest heaving. "Toraan."

"Yes?" I bent and nipped at her earlobe, which elicited another moan.

"Is that your tail between my legs?"

"Mmhmm." I moved it up higher, the furry tip twitching in anticipation. "Do you like it?"

"Do Vandar used their tails to...?"

I sucked on her ear as my tail reached the slickness between her thighs. "The tips of our tails are almost as sensitive as our cocks, and I plan to fuck you with both."

Her knees buckled but my hold on her kept her from slipping down the glass.

"Is this what you had in mind last night?" I asked. "This is what you were thinking about when you were pleasuring yourself?"

"I'd never thought of your tail..." she began, her voice desperate. "I didn't mean to wake..."

I inhaled deeply, drinking in the scent of her warm skin, and feathering my lips across the skittering pulse in her neck. "Do not apologize. I like a female who knows what she enjoys, and is not afraid to take it."

"But I don't know," she whispered. "Not everything. I mean, I haven't done all that much, especially compared to one to your pleasurers."

I raised my head to meet her eyes. "They are not *my* pleasurers. They were only ever a distraction. I would take you over them, any day."

"Why?"

I tightened my grip around her waist. "Because you will be mine. There is nothing more arousing than the sight of mating marks on your female—at least that is what I hear." My gaze dropped to the smooth, brown skin of her chest. "I want to see them on you."

"So that it will anger the admiral?" she asked.

Was that why? I knew I had not been thinking about the enemy when I'd kissed her. Even now, my desire to see her skin etched with my marks felt more like primal possession than revenge. "Of course," I lied. I nuzzled close to her neck, but my lips hovered over her skin. "This is what you want, too, isn't it? Safety with the Vandar as my mate?"

She nodded, but I wanted to hear her say it.

"Tell me you want me to claim you, Rachael," I murmured. "Tell me you want me to fuck you until you get my marks."

She sucked in a breath. "I want you." The words spilled out of her. "I want you to fuck me, Toraan."

I growled low before devouring her mouth with my own again. Her body pulsed as my tongue swirled with hers, stroking deep as I ground my hips into her. Moving my hand down from the small of her back, I slipped it under the hem of her kilt. Like all Vandar, she wore nothing underneath, which meant it was easy to feel how ready she was for me. Heat throbbed between her legs, as my fingers skimmed her ass cheeks, then parted her wet folds while my tail stroked her in the front.

"You're so wet for me," I said when I broke our kiss. I slid two fingers inside her as the tip of my tail circled her bundle of nerves.

Gasping, she reared back. Then her eyes went wide. "Can anyone see us here? Your horde ships are invisible. Could they be flying right next to us and watching?"

"Don't worry," I said, my voice husky. "This is one-way glass. No one can see that my fingers and tail are fucking you."

She rocked into me, my words obviously igniting her desire as she opened her legs for me, letting me drive deeper. I released her arm overhead and she dropped it to my shoulder, digging her nails into my flesh as my tail flicked faster and my fingers stroked in and out. Her movements and her breathing became more ragged until she started to shake, her heat pulling around my fingers.

She leaned into me as she trembled with aftershocks, and I slid my fingers from her. "How do you do that? Make me come so fast?"

"I have only begun," I told her, tangling my hands in her hair and pulling her head back so I could kiss her again. Then my hands roamed her body, moving from her back to span her waist, and cupping her breasts.

I needed to feel more of her, taste more of her. I quickly unfastened her vest and slipped it over her shoulders. The air hit her exposed breasts, and the flesh around her nipples puckered, making her shiver.

"So perfect." I bent down and captured one tight peak in my mouth.

She clamped her hands on my shoulders as I lavished attention on first one hard nipple and then the other, my mouth hot and urgent. Then I was aware of her fumbling with my shoulder armor.

I helped her by unhooking the buckles, and the leather and metal clattered to the floor. My stomach tightened when she ran both hands down my now-bare chest, and her fingers slipped beneath the belt holding up my battle kilt.

"I need to taste you," I tugged at her kilt and it finally slipped off her hips and hit the floor.

Before she could step out of it, I'd scooped her up and carried her to the bed, dropping her on it so that she bounced a few times. Staring down at her completely naked, I let out a low rumble in the back of my throat.

I expected her to be shy, lying spread out in front of me like she was, but she wasn't. Her gaze never left mine as she smiled mischievously and let her legs fall open just a bit.

With a growl, I took her ankles and jerked her to the edge of the bed, spreading her knees and dropping down. Nestling my face between her legs, I nipped at the skin on the inside of her thigh. As much as I wanted to fuck her, I loved hearing her moans of pleasure and tasting her arousal on my tongue.

Rachael arched her back as I dragged my tongue through her, parting her folds and finding her slick little nub again. She fisted the sheets as I sucked her, wrapping her legs around my back like she'd done the night before. I licked her until she was writhing and bucking against me. This time was even faster, and she screamed as she came.

When her quivering slowed, I stood and dropped my kilt. Even though Rachael's eyes were half-lidded with pleasure, her eyes widened as I stroked a hand down my cock, pumping it as I teased her opening with my tail.

I lowered myself so that I hovered over her, bracing myself on one arm. "Are you ready for me?"

She licked her bottom lip and nodded.

I kissed her, my tongue delving deep as my body pressed against hers and I moved my tail out of the way, so I could notch my cock at her opening.

Rachael drew in a breath before my mouth was over hers, subduing her cries as I pushed hard inside her. Wrapping her arms around my back, she scratched at me as I buried my cock as deep as it could go. I dragged my cock out, my crown teasing her.

"You are mine now." I thrust inside her and she gasped. "You belong to Raas Toraan of the Vandar. Do you understand?"

"Yes," she said as she panted for breath.

"Now I'm going to fuck you until your body understands, as well."

Rachael hooked her legs around my waist, her hips moving to pull me closer. Her hunger for me made me move even faster. I had been right. She was better than any pleasurer. Not because she was so skilled, but because she was so unafraid to chase her own pleasure. When she detonated a moment later, her body spasming as she arched her back, it was all I could do to hold on.

I buried my head in her neck as I hammered home, my strokes long and fast as her body clenched my cock like a vise. Rachael's hands slipped as she tried to grasp my slick back, my muscles bunched beneath her fingers, and after a final thrust, I exploded inside her, holding myself deep and finally collapsing on the bed beside her.

CHAPTER 23

Rachael

My body was jelly as I tried to catch my breath. Raas Toraan's breathing was heavy, his chest rising and falling as he lay next to me on his back. His tail was draped across his corded stomach, and even *it* looked spent. I rested my hand on the dark fur at the tip, stroking it slowly as my heartbeat attempted to return to normal.

After a few moments, he rolled his head to face me. "You wish for more?"

I gaped at him. "Right now?" I wasn't sure if I could survive another release like the ones he'd just given me.

"If you continue to stimulate my tail, I will need to fuck you again—and soon."

My fingers stilled, and I retracted my hand. "Sorry. I forgot your tail was *that* sensitive."

Toraan rolled over toward me. "Do not apologize. I enjoy your hands on my tail, but it makes me want to do things with it that you might not be ready for."

I didn't think my body could heat any more than it already had, but I felt a fresh pulse of warmth bloom across my cheeks. "And using your tail is not considered one of those fetishes you mentioned?"

One of his dark eyebrows twitched. "Not for a Vandar."

Even though we'd just been as physically close as two beings could be, I was struck by how little I knew him and his people. "There wasn't much talk of the Vandar on Horl."

"Your planet is controlled by the Zagrath. They would not want you to know about us, except the disinformation they wish to spread."

As much as I'd loved growing up on Horl, being away from it was making me realize how little I'd known about it and especially about the wider galaxy. My life on my home world had seemed idyllic, if sheltered and controlled, but I'd never known anything else. I thought females everywhere needed to dress to cover their skin and be quiet in the presence of males. The empire was universally accepted as our generous benefactors, and the Vandar were bloodthirsty monsters bent on destroying and killing without care.

"Does it bother you?" I asked.

"Does what bother me?"

"That the empire says such awful things about your people." I met his eyes. "You aren't like how they describe you."

"No? How are we different?" His hazel eyes flashed. "How am I different?"

"You aren't as scary as I expected. I thought you'd tear your enemy apart with your bare hands and feast on their blood. And I imagined a Raas would have a harem of females to which you'd do depraved things."

He laughed. "I did not know our reputation outmatched our lust for battle and females."

I frowned at him. "Are you making fun of me?"

"No, but I am shocked you ever set foot off your transport, if you believed us to be such monsters. Did you fear being thrown into my harem?"

I shrugged. "Kind of. I didn't know that the Vandar didn't have females on their ships, and I knew nothing of mating marks."

He flicked a hand toward the room. "You can see that I have no harem, and so far, I have served you no flesh from our enemies."

"Does it bother you that the Zagrath say such things about you?"

His expression darkened for a moment. "The only way the Zagrath can justify their illegal actions is to make those of us who fight against them and for freedom into the enemy. We do not go after garrisons that are not imperial, nor to we raid ships unaffiliated with the empire. Those planets we have liberated know who we are. The people who now live without the imperial yoke around their necks have seen the truth. That is enough for us."

I couldn't help the rush of pride I felt. Raas Toraan was far from anything I'd expected. Even though I didn't know him well, I knew he was a better creature than the Zagrath admiral. "I'm glad your ship intercepted me."

"As am I."

"I'd take anything over being married off to Admiral Kurmog," I said, the words rushing out before I could think about them.

He stiffened. "Yes, it was fortuitous for both of us. Without you, we never would have known about the empire's search for our colonies."

His tone had shifted, and he was now the strategic warlord who had made the deal, and not the passionate Vandar who had trembled in my arms as he'd bellowed his pleasure.

"I didn't mean— "

He pushed himself up before I could finish. "I know what you meant. This was a good move for both of us. We should keep our objective in mind."

His sharp words stung, and I swallowed back tears. Why had I said that? When I'd escaped from the Zagrath ship, I *had* been willing to take anything over marriage to the admiral, but that did not mean I saw the Raas as something barely better than the alternative. Not anymore.

He swung his legs over the side of the bed and stood quickly. "I should return to my inventory of the ship."

I sat up and tracked him as he strode naked toward the bathroom. "Do you really have to go?"

He didn't glance over at me, but instead, looked down at his bare chest. "I will return. Mating marks do not appear so easily."

The thought that he would be back because he needed to mark me as part of his plan made me pull the dark, silky sheets up around my chest. The tears clouding my vision blurred the sight of his hard body as he disappeared through the arched doorway.

Stop being such a baby, I told myself as I blinked rapidly. You never wanted to fall in love with a Vandar. You never wanted to fall in love with anyone. You just wanted to escape a loveless marriage and experience more than your cloistered life on Horl had allowed.

"Well, you got your wish," I said under my breath.

Splashing noises told me that the Raas was bathing himself, but even though I would have liked to watch or even slip in the steaming water with him, I remained in bed. He was right. I shouldn't get carried away just because he felt so right inside me. This was a Raas of the Vandar, who was used to being with two females at a time on these pleasure planets. He barely knew me, after all. He wasn't going to fall for a human who'd only ever been with a stable boy and couldn't even imagine half the things he probably did with his tail.

My pulse quickened. As much as the alien warlord with the huge cock and skillful tail aroused me, I needed to focus on keeping my emotions in check. This was about sex and strategy. Nothing more. Fucking him was what I needed to do to get his mating marks and keep me out of Zagrath hands. He'd been clear about that from the beginning.

But that didn't mean I couldn't enjoy it. A lot.

CHAPTER 24

Toraan

"We're loading the shuttles now, Raas." My *majak* joined me on the command deck as I observed the planet we orbited out the front view screen.

I grunted in acknowledgment. Our raiders had descended to the surface—several shuttles from each horde warbird—and after securing the needed supplies for our journey, we'd gotten a transmission that they were loading up and preparing to return. There was no need to stay any longer than needed. The planet of T'Ploc was a small, class-M planet with an arid climate and frequent windstorms.

I eyed the beige surface covered with swirling clouds of the same color. Not much grew in the planet's soil, so its natives had become skilled at acquiring supplies from other worlds and then redistributing them to those wishing to stay off the empire's radar. It was not the first time we'd resupplied at T'Ploc, and I doubted it would be the last.

"We found everything we need?" I asked, scraping a hand through my damp hair.

"Everything but wine and females."

I choked back a laugh. "We will find neither of those on this rock." The natives of T'Ploc were tall, spindly, hairless creatures with bulbous eyes that never blinked. My raiders were not yet horny enough to desire *these* aliens.

"Incoming ship, Raas." One of my command deck warriors turned from his console.

"Identifier?" I asked, as Rolan shifted beside me.

We both watched as a hulking, gray ship came into view. It was massive, but it was no warship. I spotted no externally mounted weapons, and it moved slower than was optimal for any kind of tactical vessel.

The warrior returned his gaze to his console, tapping and swiping quickly. "Doloran. No significant weapon capability and limited defenses." He let out a small sigh. "They're hailing us."

"Doloran?" My *majak's* voice brimmed with curiosity. "Are we truly this lucky?"

I clasped my hands behind me and rocked back on my heels. "On screen."

The view screen flickered, and then the image of the dusty planet was replaced with a stunning female. She sat on a gilded captain's chair, surrounded by cushions in sumptuous jewel tones. White-blonde hair cascaded down her shoulders in elaborate braids, and the sheerest of fabrics covered her lush body, pale-blue skin showing through the gossamer.

Rolan emitted a growl, and several other command deck warriors made low noises of hungry approval.

"The Vandar," the female purred as she sat forward and smiled seductively.

"I am Raas Toraan of the Vandar. And you are...?"

"Silaria of the pleasure ship Conkarra." Her smile widened. "At your service, Raas."

"You are all Doloran?" My *majak* asked. The Doloran were known throughout the galaxy for their throats that could expand and contract at will, a fact that was not lost on a single member of my command deck crew.

Silaria shifted her gaze to him and lifted a perfectly arched eyebrow. "Not all, but many. I assure you that we have enough variety to satisfy even a horde of Vandar raiders."

"Raas?" Rolan's voice was low and he did not turn toward me. "This would save us an extra stop."

"You would be willing to forgo an entire pleasure planet?" I asked, matching his volume.

"I think I speak for the crew when I say yes."

I cut my eyes to Rolan. "Has it really been so long?"

"If you have to ask, then I know you are enjoying your new mate, Raas."

I did not respond to this, memories of how I'd left Rachael filling me with regret. I should not have reacted like I did. She was only being honest, and I was being unfair if I expected her motivations to change just because I'd made her cry out in pleasure a few times.

It was more than that, I thought. It was more than how eagerly her body responded to mine or how good it felt to be lodged deep inside her. There was something more. Something I had never felt with the many pleasurers I'd fucked. Something I didn't want to think about.

"Raas?" Rolan asked. "What is your decision? Should we dock with the Conkarra?"

I flicked my hand at the warrior controlling the transmission—a signal to silence the audio—and turned my head to my *majak*. "Do a sweep of the ship to make sure there is no trace that they've been in contact with the empire, and obviously, no imperial soldiers. I do not want to walk into a trap with our cocks hanging out."

It was not common, but in the past, the empire had used pleasure ships to ambush their enemy. It was one of the reasons I preferred pleasure planets with clear neutrality.

Rolan's mouth twitched. "Yes, Raas. It is done."

"Once it's clear, the Conkarra may dock with us, and send transports to the other horde ships."

"The crew will be pleased, Raas." He hesitated before speaking again. "Will you require a pleasurer for yourself? I could arrange for her to join you in your strategy room, if—"

I waved a hand to cut him off. "No. I will leave the Doloran and their talents all to you and the other raiders. But I will be in my strategy room reviewing the latest intelligence reports, and intercepted imperial transmissions."

"Understood, Raas."

I signaled to my warrior to resume the audio transmission, then pivoted to the screen where the female pleasurer sat patiently, her smile unwavering. "You and your ladies are welcome on our warbirds."

She inclined her head at me. "We are most grateful, Raas." She ran her tongue slowly across her bottom lip. "I look forward to thanking you personally."

"No need. As long as my raiders are happy, that is enough." I nodded to Rolan. "My *majak* will discuss the procedure and your compensation."

Silaria leaned forward, exposing an ample amount of light-blue cleavage. "As you wish, Raas."

I nodded to Rolan, his heels clicking together as I walked off the command deck and through the door to the side that led to my strategy room. The smaller compartment was comforting after the buzz of the command deck, and I sat down behind my massive, ebony desk.

The arrival of the pleasure ship had not taken my mind off Rachael, as it should have. Seeing the seductive pleasurer had only done the opposite—fuel my desire for the human. My heart pounded and my cock sprang to life as I let my thoughts wander to Rachael.

I slammed a hand on my desk, the sharp sting clearing my mind. I could not let my feelings get away from me. I needed to focus on the deal I'd made with her, and nothing else. I knew all too well the pain that came from feeling too much for someone who did not feel the same way. Rachael had agreed to be my mate to avoid marrying an old man. Not because she loved me. How could she? She had known nothing of me when she'd agreed to the deal—only that it was her only option to stay out of the clutches of the admiral.

I had agreed to take her as my mate to protect her and inflict humiliation on the empire. If I was feeling more for her—a pull and desire I'd never experienced before—then I needed to control my emotions and remember that this was only strategy. I thought back to her spread out beneath me—her legs open and her smile teasing—and I groaned. Was that even possible?

CHAPTER 25

Rachael

I'd waited until Toraan had bathed and dressed before getting up, even though he'd been so fast and distracted as pulled on his kilt and strapped on his armor that I doubted he would have noticed if I'd pranced by him completely naked. Once he'd gone —pausing briefly to look at me still wrapped in the sheet and tell me gruffly that he'd be back to dine with me—I'd slipped from bed and padded into the bathroom.

Even though he'd bathed quickly, the room remained pristine, with a thick-weave mat next to the pools, and an ivory towel draped near the steps. Lowering myself into the hot water, I groaned as the heat enveloped me. I closed my eyes and tried to let the tension of the last few days dissolve, but my mind kept returning to Toraan's swift departure from bed.

Why did I have to mention Kurmog? What male wants to hear that the only reason you're with them is so you wouldn't have to screw an old man?

"Apparently not Toraan," I muttered to myself.

The truth was, I didn't know how to be around males. I'd been kept from them for most of my life, so I had no experience in how to flatter them or even just talk to them. Talking had not been high on my agenda when I'd dragged the horse master's assistant to the hayloft, and he hadn't cared about being charmed. But if I was going to be this Vandar's mate, I needed to figure things out fast, or I was going to spend a lot of time watching him stalk away from me.

After a while of bobbing in the water worrying and letting my fingers prune, the doors outside swished open. I swiped water from my eyes as I blinked rapidly. He was back already?

I started to stand up, then I stopped. Maybe I should stay in the pool and invite him to join me. It would be easier than talking to him and trying to explain what I'd meant earlier.

"I'm in here," I called out. "You should come on in."

"Indeed?"

The figure that appeared in the arched doorway was not Toraan. It was a female. A striking female, with pale-blue skin, and platinum-blonde hair.

I dipped even lower under the surface of the pool, although she could not see any part of me in the crimson water. "Who are you?"

"Silaria." She appraised me openly. "Who are you?"

"I'm Rachael." Then I added with a measure of defiance. "I'm Raas Toraan's mate."

Her gray eyes widened, not in shock, but in some sort of approval. "I am pleased to meet you." She stepped closer, her sheer, dark-blue gown fluttering behind her. "Are you Zagrath? Has the Raas captured a Zagrath and made her his mate?"

"I'm not Zagrath." It took effort not to snap. "I'm human from the planet Horl."

This Silaria did not appear to notice my sharp tone. "You're quite beautiful for a human. I have not seen one of you with such lovely, brown skin."

"Thank you." Even though she was flattering me, I was not comfortable with this creature waltzing into the Raas' quarters and asking me questions. "Why are you here? There are no other females on the ship."

"That is true." She almost floated over to the long counter and hopped onto it, her long legs swinging below her and easily seen through the diaphanous fabric of her dress. "I am the captain of a pleasure ship called the Conkarra."

"Pleasure ship?" Toraan had mentioned pleasure planets, but there were pleasure *ships*, as well?

"It is our first time servicing this horde, but we are no stranger to the Vandar. My ladies love raiders." She gave me a knowing look. "I'm sure you would agree that they are quite enjoyable."

I was glad the heat of the water would mask any flush to my skin, but I dropped my gaze from her intense one.

"Horl," she said. "I've heard of your planet, although I'm sure I've never recruited a pleasurer from there."

I nearly choked back a laugh. "A pleasurer from Horl? Not likely."

She nodded, narrowed her eyes. "So how did a human from a sexually repressive planet manage to snag herself a gorgeous Raas of the Vandar?"

I had a strange urge to defend Horl, but she was right. And her question was not a bad one. "We made a deal."

Her brows rose. "A deal? How intriguing." She leaned forward. "Tell me about it."

"You still haven't told me why you're here. And not on this ship—in the Raas' quarters."

She smiled at me. "Clearly, I came here to offer myself to the Raas as a thank you for allowing us to dock with his horde. I had no idea he had a mate." Her gaze drifted down from my eyes. "But no mating marks."

I slid lower in the water. "Not yet. We just… I mean, I haven't been on the ship for long."

"I see." She tapped one slender finger on her chin. "In that case, I have a proposition for you."

I did not like the sound of that, especially if it meant sharing Toraan with her. My face must have shown my discomfort because she let out a peal of laughter.

"I have no intention of stealing your Vandar from you. But since I won't be pleasuring him, I'd like to offer to teach you."

"Teach me?"

She tilted her head and inclined it slightly. "You're very beautiful, but if you come from Horl, I doubt you know much about what pleases a Vandar."

Well, she was right about that. Most of what we'd done had been Toraan pleasing me, and although I wasn't about to complain about it, it would be nice to return the favor.

"Do Vandar like different things than other males?" I asked.

She shrugged one bare shoulder. "Males are not so complicated, but there are differences between species."

"Like the tails," I said.

"Exactly. If you can use a Vandar's tail properly it can bring you both pleasure." She leaned forward, gathering the hem of her skirt and making it into a fabric facsimile of a tail. "The tip is where you want to concentrate. Not only is it sensitive, the Vandar can manipulate it like a hand."

I watched her in rapt fascination as she stroked the fabric bunched above her fist.

"Long steady strokes with your hand squeezing the base of the furry tip is a good way to start," she continued. "You can put it in your mouth, but that's a lot of fur to swallow. Personally, I'd rather suck his cock and ride his tail."

"Ride his tail?" My voice cracked on the last word.

"Mmhmm. You haven't lived until you've been tail-fucked by a Vandar." Her eyelids fluttered as she let out a breathy sigh. "I'd also say you haven't lived until you've experienced a night with a two-phallused Tenniren, but let's not rush you."

I gaped at her. I'd never been around a female who talked like this. Of course, I'd never actually met a female who exchanged sexual favors for money.

She caught my expression and laughed. "Too much?"

Considering everything I'd learned over the past few days, I guessed learning sex tips from an alien prostitute shouldn't have been any more shocking than discovering that the Vandar weren't actually the bad guys.

"It's okay," I said. "I'd like to make the Raas happy in bed, even if our arrangement is political."

Silaria shook her head. "I doubt a Vandar male would have taken you to his bed for only political reasons, even a Raas who is known for his clever strategy. But if you want to make him even more pleased with his decision, you should become skilled with your mouth."

"You mean kissing?"

Silaria uncrossed her legs and swung herself down from the counter. "I mean deepthroating, darling. Like I said before, tails are tricky because of all the fur, but if you can learn to take one of their huge cocks down your throat, he'll love you forever."

I wanted to explain that neither Toraan or I were in this for love and certainly not forever, but I was too stuck on the idea of trying to take Toraan's cock in my mouth to utter a word. Was she serious? That thing was massive.

Silaria didn't wait for me to reply before perching on the stone wall of the pool. "Of course, Dolorans are at an advantage because we have expandable throats and no gag impulse, but even a human can learn some tricks that will drive your Vandar wild."

"I'm pretty sure my mouth doesn't even open that wide," I said.

She fluttered her blue fingers at me. "I'm sure you can with a little practice, but don't forget that you also have your tongue and fingers to work with." She reached into the water and grabbed my arm, pulling it out and holding it close to her mouth. "Watch and learn, sweetie."

CHAPTER 26

Toraan

The walkways were almost entirely deserted, as I made my way through the ship from my strategy room. The pleasure ship Conkarra had departed, and with it all the females who had filled my warbird with the sounds of merriment and ecstasy. There were no more scantily clad Dolorans, swishing through the corridors with warriors close on their heels, or Vandar with females kneeling in front of them, their heads buried beneath battle kilts. The pleasurers had been compensated, and we had resumed our course for Zendaren, with most of the crew either passed out from exhaustion, or smiling widely as they manned their posts.

I leapt over the last two steps of a spiraling staircase, rattling the steel floor as I landed. While my raiders had been busy enjoying themselves, I'd remained in my strategy room, studying my star charts and reviewing every intercepted transmission from the empire. The work had calmed me, and reassured me that the Zagrath did not have any concrete information regarding our secret colonies. They might be reasonably certain of their existence, but there was no indication they had pinpointed a location, or even narrowed down their search. The galaxy was endless, and we'd been hiding our people for a millennium.

"You can keep looking," I muttered darkly to myself. "You won't find them."

Working had also kept my mind off the female in my quarters. Or at least, distracted me a bit. As much as I had tried to focus on the maps and readouts, my thoughts had continued to drift back to her—and to what she'd said.

I needed to remember exactly what this was—a military decision—and not let myself be carried away by how beautiful she was, or how good she felt. I'd taken her as my mate, but as a strategic move. Not to fall for her.

"So much for that."

I reached the doorway to my quarters and pressed a palm on the panel to open them. I fully expected her to be asleep and to slip into bed next to her. As I'd thought, the room was dim and quiet. I slipped off my armor by the door, kicked off my boots, and stepped out of my battle kilt and belt.

"I've been waiting for you, Raas."

The soft voice halted my steps toward the bed and drew my gaze to the figure sitting up against the backboard. "I did not expect you to be awake."

"Like I said, I've been waiting." She let the dark sheet fall from her chest. "And Silaria left a while ago."

That name made my mouth drop open. Silaria was the madam of the pleasure ship. The one who'd offered herself to me. "She was here?"

Rachael nodded as she kicked the sheets off to reveal her naked body. "She was pretty interesting. I've never talked to a pleasurer before."

I didn't know what to say to that, but I was very aware that my cock was hardening at the sight of the human moving to the end of the bed on her hands and knees. Her shyness seemed to have vanished, along with any traces of the sheltered female from Horl.

She curled one of her fingers, beckoning me. Speech failed me, but I walked forward until I was standing in front of her.

Tipping her head back, she licked her lips and smiled as she ran one hand down my chest, bumping along the ridges of my stomach.

Her touch made my cock even harder, and it jutted out stiff from my body. She wrapped her fingers around it, and I let out a moan as she moved her hand up the length of it. She traced the tip of her finger around the crown, sliding across the moisture beading at the tip.

I closed my eyes to keep from exploding, then opened them instantly when I felt her tongue on me. The sight of her pink tongue swirling around the head of my cock caused me to moan again.

She peered up at me, pausing long enough to ask if I liked what she was doing.

I nodded, trying to find coherent words. "Did Silaria tell you how to do this?"

She nodded, returning her lips to my cock and taking the head into her mouth. My eyes almost rolled into the back of my head as she sucked hard, and I tangled my fingers in her hair. Not only was she sucking my cock, she was on all fours doing it, her back arched and her round ass high in the air. *Tvek.* I should have paid the madam even more than she'd requested.

Rachael kept her fist tight around the base of my cock, sliding it up and down as she sucked. I tightened my grip in her hair, trying to control the overwhelming sensations wracking my body.

She looked up again as she spread her legs slightly. "I want your tail."

I stared at her for a moment, not sure I'd heard what I thought I had. "You want me to…?"

Her pupils flared. "Fuck me with your tail while I suck you."

My body jerked. Had the innocent female from Horl really just asked me to tail fuck her? She gave me a mischievous smile and wiggled her ass before she returned her mouth to my cock.

I didn't ask her again, my possessive and dominant Vandar instinct taking over. I bent my tail under her body, sliding it between her breasts and down her stomach until I reached her folds. She quivered as my furry tip parted her and stroked up and down.

When I found her slick nub and circled it, it was her turn to jerk. Even though her mouth was filled with my cock, she moaned, the muffled noise vibrating down my shaft. I kept swirling my tail until she started to tremble, her noises getting more desperate even as she kept her lips stretched around my cock.

As she detonated, I slid my tail lower and thrust it inside her, her body clenching hard as she rocked into me. I didn't wait, but dragged it out and in again as she came, my pace relentless as my tail fucked her hard.

She pulled my cock from her mouth just long enough to gasp. "Your tail feels so good."

"Not as good as your mouth feels sucking me," I growled, as she curled her fingers around my girth and stretched her lips around the thick head of my cock again. Watching her mouth on me while my tail was snug inside her tight cunt made my heart thunder in my chest and the blood rush hot in my ears.

She was so tight, and her mouth was so wet and hot. I grunted as I used my hand on the back of her head to pull her even closer, captivated by watching her suck me down. Knowing she was my mate somehow made it even hotter, and knowing she'd never done this for another male sent a possessive thrill through me.

"Your pretty little mouth is all mine." I pushed my tail deeper inside her, the nerve endings practically vibrating. "So is this sweet little cunt."

Her pace quickened, and she made a keening noise that made me bite my lip.

"Rachael," I rasped. "I can't hold back any longer."

She reached one hand around and grabbed my bare ass, pulling me until my cock bumped the back of her throat. With a roar, I threw back my head and pulsed into her mouth.

After a moment, I looked down and saw Rachael swallowing and dabbing at her mouth. "That was even better than Silaria said it would be."

My legs shook as her fingers released my cock. "Maybe we should dock with more pleasure ships."

She twitched one shoulder up. "Or maybe you should spend more time with your mate, so you can discover what other tricks I learned."

Any hope I'd had of not falling for the human female had officially flown out the window, along with my self-control.

CHAPTER 27

Rachael

I was surprised how much I'd loved sucking Toraan, and how much I'd gotten turned on by having his tail inside me. Sex was nothing like my mother had said, and was even better than my inexperienced fumbling in the stables back on Horl. Even though I'd agreed to the deal with the Raas for different reasons, it was easy to forget that fact. More than once, as I was curled up next to him in bed, I had to remind myself that Toraan was spending so much time with me for a purpose.

It was no hardship to spend the rest of the journey in bed with him, although he did leave our quarters occasionally to check on the ship's progress, and ensure the Zagrath weren't in pursuit. Rotations passed in a blur, with our meals being delivered and sometimes uneaten, as we couldn't seem to get enough of each other. But as much time as we spent with our limbs entwined and our skin glistening with sweat, mating marks had still not appeared for either one of us. Toraan never mentioned it, but I'd caught him glancing down at his bare chest a few times.

"Are you hungry?" He called out from the main room as I lowered myself into the second level of the pools, the slightly warm, orange water bubbling up around me and releasing a spicy scent. The hot water below was too hot for my tender flesh, especially after being pounded over and over by the Raas. Even alternating between his cock and his furry tail had not prevented the soreness that made me walk gingerly.

"Starving," I yelled back, inhaling the perfume of the water and letting my muscles uncoil. "I'll be out in a little while."

I leaned my head against the stone ledge and stretched my arms behind me. I wasn't sure what was in the orange water, but it definitely helped lessen my soreness. If it hadn't been for my frequent soaks I doubted I would have been able to walk at all.

Water splashing over the side made me open my eyes. Toraan was stepping into the water, his long, thick cock swinging between his legs and drawing my gaze. As much time as I'd spent up close and personal with it, I still couldn't help staring.

"I thought we were recuperating," he said, catching my eyes and giving me a look of mock surprise.

"We are. I am." I splashed him as he sank down next to me in the water, then closed my eyes again. "You're the one who's insatiable."

He choked out a laugh. "Says the human who woke me up this morning by straddling me."

"If you don't want me to touch you, you shouldn't get so hard in the mornings."

"All males wake up with hard cocks."

I opened one eye and peeked at him. "Really?"

This time he laughed fully. "I have never heard of a species where the males did not."

My face warmed. There was still so much I didn't know about males, and especially Vandar males. Sometimes I wished I'd had more time with the alien madam. "Then I'll try not to pester you in the mornings."

"I didn't say you were pestering me." He tugged me so that I was sitting on his lap and wrapped his arms around me, his body cocooning mine from behind. "I've never enjoyed waking up so much in my life."

I smiled and leaned my head so that it rested on his shoulder. "Same here. I wish we could stay like this forever."

"Since you agreed to be my mate, and I have no intention of leaving the horde or sending you off the ship, you will get your wish."

"Until we reach the Vandar colony," I reminded him. I didn't know why, but I got a nervous flutter in my stomach every time I thought about visiting one of the secret colonies and meeting Vandar who weren't part of Raas Toraan's horde.

"We will not be on Zendaren for long." He used his large hands to scoop water onto my exposed chest, the bubbles tickling my skin as they popped. "I will meet with my uncle to discuss strategy and defenses for the colonies now that the Zagrath suspect their existence, and my raiders will see their family. We also have several warriors who will be taking mates on Zendaren and leaving the horde."

"Do I need to come to the surface, or can I stay here and wait for you?"

"The entire horde will land on Zendaren." He cupped my breasts in his hands and thumbed my nipples. "I will be introducing you to my uncle, the former Raas. He will want to see the female I have taken as a mate."

"Will you tell him?"

"That I am obsessed with your perfect body and your sweet little cunt?" His words were dark and low as his lips buzzed my ear. "No, I think I'll keep that to myself."

I wanted to elbow him, but his touch was making it hard to concentrate. Already my nipples were hard points, and I wiggled in his lap as his cock swelled beneath me. "You know what I mean, Toraan."

"The only person on Zendaren I would consider telling is my uncle, and only because our arrangement is part of the larger strategy with the empire."

My heart sank a little bit. "Of course."

"You do not need to worry about Raas Maassen. He will be as charmed by you as I was."

I twisted around in his lap to face him. "He won't be bothered that I'm human?"

"He was always a progressive Raas, who understood the need of our hordes to adapt. He is not a purist like my father." He smoothed one of my curls away from my face and tucked it behind one ear. "And I do not care what anyone else on Zendaren thinks of my decision. I am a Raas, and I have chosen you. It is done."

"Does saying that always work?"

"Saying what?"

"It is done."

He grinned. "I have never given it much thought. It is what we say when something is settled."

"And we're settled?"

His eyes held mine. "Have I not said you are my mate?"

I nodded. "I guess it's done."

He leaned forward and brushed his lips across mine. "It is."

I was soaking in the scented water to heal my aching flesh, but being so close to Toraan made hunger flare within me. No matter how much he fucked me, I could not get enough of him. I moaned and returned his kiss.

Even as he shifted me forward so that his cock was notched at my opening, I wasn't sure if I felt reassured. It was one thing to give a human asylum, and take her as a mate to protect her when you were flying around in a horde. It was another to bring a human mate to a colony of Vandar.

I pushed my worries from my mind as I braced my hands on his shoulders, lifting myself so that I could sink down onto his rigid length and start to ride. I was so lost in our mutual moans of pleasure and water sloshing over the stone ledge that I didn't hear the thumping of the door until Toraan's *majak* was standing outside the bathroom doorway, loudly clearing his throat.

"We have arrived, Raas," he said, when we'd stopped moving and I'd buried my head in Toraan's shoulder. "You asked me to alert you immediately. The horde is in orbit above Zendaren."

CHAPTER 28

Toraan

"I apologize for disturbing you in your quarters, Raas, but you did insist I notify you when—"

I waved away Rolan's words as we entered the command deck, the steel doors gliding open upon our approach. "I did want to know. You were correct to alert me."

My skin was still damp from the bathing pools, the scent of the perfumed water lingering, even though I'd quickly toweled off. I'd brushed my hair off my shoulders, but the damp ends dripped down my bare back. At least I'd remembered my armor and battle axe in my rush to jump out of the pool and get dressed.

Rachael was probably still sitting in the water in shock that I'd run out in such a hurry, but I hoped she would soon be getting dressed. She knew we'd arrived and would be going to the surface together—even if the prospect made her nervous.

There was a different energy when I stepped onto the command deck. All my warriors were at their posts, but they stood taller and stared more intently at the view screen. My eyes were also drawn to the wide wall of glass, and the planet we hovered above.

Zendaren. One of the secret Vandar colonies.

I let out a breath when I saw it, as if releasing a lifetime of nomadic wandering in the air that left my lips. "We're here."

The planet was as blue as I'd remembered, deep oceans covering much of the surface, but there was a large swath of land in the center, and islands spread across the sea. The heart of the colony was on the largest parcel of land—a mix of open plains and green forests, with rivers and streams running through it. From our high orbit, I couldn't see the details of the Vandar city or the villages that had grown up around it, but I knew it was there beneath the clouds.

It had taken our ancestors many rotations to find planets far enough away from Zagrath territory and similar enough to the Vandar home world to appeal to our people. Zendaren was the first, but there were others. Much as we had many hordes in space, we'd learned never to concentrate our resources in one place. The more we were spread out, the harder it would be for the enemy to find us and wipe out our civilization.

"Report," I said, my voice cracking as I drank in the sight of the first home I'd known.

"Zendaren appears to be as it always is, Raas." One of my warriors pivoted toward me. "Defense patrols are in place, and there are still no incoming ships on our long-range sensors."

Viken joined me and Rolan overlooking the command deck and the view screen. "We were not followed."

I gave him a sharp nod, relieved to hear his confident assessment. "I'm assuming we have given our approach codes to the security patrol?"

"Affirmative, Raas. We have been hailed."

My heart beat a bit faster. "On screen."

Within moments, the image of the planet flickered and disappeared, replaced by one of an elder Vandar, silver streaking his dark hair. My uncle.

I immediately clicked my heels together, as did the rest of the command deck crew. "Raas Maassen."

The old Raas inclined his head just a touch, before a grin split his face. "You are Raas now, Toraan."

"Old habits die hard," I told him, returning the smile.

I was happier to see him than I'd even suspected, my heart squeezing at the sight of the Vandar who had practically raised me, and taught me how to be a warrior and a Raas. He had aged since I'd last been on Zendaren, his wrinkles deeper and his hair more silvered, but his eyes retained their intensity.

"It is a surprise to see you," he said, "although not a bad one."

"I felt it was time for my raiders to see their families." I clasped my hands behind my back. "We also have several Vandar who wish to take mates and retire their battle axes."

I did not want to tell him about the admiral or that the enemy was aware we had secret Vandar colonies. That would wait until I could talk with him in person, as would the revelation that I'd taken a human mate.

My uncle nodded, as if accepting this answer, but his eyes held mine for a moment longer. "Very well. We welcome you and your horde back to Zendaren."

I bowed my head slightly. "Thank you. We are eager for a rest from the skies."

"And I am hungry for tales of battle." He leaned forward. "I hope you are not opposed to a celebration feast in your horde's honor."

Both my *majak* and battle chief shifted beside me. There were no banquets like the ones held on Zendaren, and I knew both warriors were eager to drink and eat with our kinsmen—and enjoy a meal not prepared from dry rations.

"We would be honored," I answered for my crew.

"Good." Raas Maassen sat back. "If you drop your invisibility shielding, our patrols will escort your horde to the surface."

"It is done." I tipped my head to Viken, who ordered shielding to be dropped as the transmission ended and my uncle's face vanished from the screen and the planet reappeared.

"The Raas looks good," Rolan said, as we watched a squadron of Vandar fighters flank our warbird. "Zendaren suits him."

I grunted in agreement. I'd never considered leaving my post as Raas, especially because I'd never harbored the idea of taking a mate and returning to one of the colonies to either raise a family or rest. My vision for my life had always included leading my horde until I died in battle. It had been easy to choose a raider's life—and death—when there was no one who would miss you, or no one you cared enough to miss. My thoughts drifted to Rachael. Did I still have no reason to choose a different path?

"What are your orders, Raas?"

I twisted my head to Rolan, realizing I had not heard the entirety of his question.

He must have seen my momentary confusion because he repeated his question. "Do you wish to leave a patrol on board the ship, or do all raiders get leave?"

"We do not need a security patrol while we are on Zendaren. The entire horde should partake in the celebration banquet."

"May I notify the crew?" Viken asked.

I couldn't help smiling at him. It had been a long time since our horde had enjoyed a true Vandar banquet. "By all means."

As my battle chief went to his post to transmit the news throughout the ship, Rolan cleared his throat. "You did not mention the human to Raas Maassen. Do you not plan to bring her with us?"

"Of course, I do." My pulse quickened. "But I did not feel it was something to mention in a transmission. It will be better if the Raas meets her first."

"So her beauty can sway him?"

I wished I felt confident that Raas Maassen would be swayed by beauty, but I knew him better than that. He was a seasoned Vandar raider who lived and breathed strategy, and who never took action without assessing the long-term effects. He also knew my mind as well as anyone, and knew that he'd trained me to be several steps ahead of my enemy. He would understand that my strategy with Rachael was a clever tactical move.

I swallowed hard, my throat tight. Then why did I feel such trepidation at the thought of going to the surface and seeing my uncle and mentor? Why did the sight of Zendaren fill my heart with dread?

CHAPTER 29

Rachael

"Are you sure I'm okay like this?" I stood next to Toraan as we waited for the warbird to touch down on the planet. I was wearing the only outfit I had—the fabric kilt and sleeveless vest—but I wished I'd insisted they save my wedding dress. At least, that would have made more of an impression. In my rumpled, ill-fitting clothes, it was hard to feel like I was going to impress anyone.

"Of course."

Since he hadn't looked at me, I put one hand on my hip. "As long as all the Vandar women go topless, as well."

That got his attention. He snapped his gaze to me—to my chest, more specifically—then frowned when he realized I'd tricked him. He let out a sigh and turned to face me. "You do not need to concern yourself with what you wear." He swiveled back around. "Besides, I will have the seamstresses on Zendaren make you an appropriate gown for the banquet."

My stomach clenched. He'd mentioned the banquet when he'd come to fetch me from his quarters, and the crew appeared to be buzzing about it. I knew it was meant to be a celebration of the horde's return to the colony, but I wasn't sure what to expect from a Vandar party. I'd been wrong in my assumptions about the raiders so far, but it was also clear to me that they knew how to enjoy themselves.

"Maybe I shouldn't go to the banquet. I'm not a Vandar, after all."

He cut his eyes to me, then curled his tail around my waist as the ship touched down and shuddered. "You are my mate, and I want you to be there."

His tone was so authoritative I didn't dare disagree with him. He was probably right. It would be weird if I spent the entire journey in bed with the Raas and then didn't go out in public with him. But I still wasn't confident that him announcing a human as his mate would go over smoothly.

I glanced over my shoulder. His *majak* and battle chief were waiting directly behind us, along with rows of raiders. Feet shifted impatiently on the steel floor as a wide ramp descended, sunlight peeking through a slat at the top. For these warriors, this was a return to the closest thing they had to a home world. For me, this was my first visit to an alien planet.

Come on, Rachael, I told myself. You can do this. You were trained for this.

As much as I'd despised being schooled in etiquette, manners, and small talk, I was now grateful that my mother had put so much emphasis on training me to finesse any situation. She'd imagined she was doing it to prepare me for life married to a top Zagrath officer, but it would come in handy now.

The ramp touched down, and Toraan slipped his tail from around my waist. He threw back his shoulders. *"Vaes,"* he said to me without looking down.

I fought the instinct to take his hand. I was sure a Raas of the Vandar did not hold hands, especially not as he descended victorious from his warbird. He strode down the ramp and I rushed forward after him, trying my best to appear regal and confident, even though I felt neither of those things.

I blinked a few times, my eyes adjusting to the bright sunlight after being on the dark ship. We'd landed on a wide stretch of hard-packed, black dirt, and the other parked horde ships surrounded us as their crews descended. There were cheers from the gathered crowd, and my breath caught in my throat as I saw just how many Vandar had crowded the shipyard to greet the returning horde. There were bodies as far as I could see, with blades thrust high in the air as they chanted.

"Holy shit," I said, before I could stop myself. Luckily, the buzz of the crowd drowned out any sound I might make. I could probably scream out a litany of curses, and no one would notice.

Raas Toraan spared me a quick glance, so maybe he heard, but he turned just as quickly back around. He stopped at the base of the ramp where a semi-circle of elaborately dressed Vandar waited.

"Raas Toraan." An older Vandar stepped forward to greet him, clapping a hand to Toraan's arm.

The Raas clicked his heels and put his own hand on the elder's other arm. "Raas Maassen."

They held each other for a moment as I held my breath, then the older alien pulled Toraan into a rough hug, thumping him hard on the back. The officers who'd been behind me moved forward, also greeting the older Vandar with clicks of their heels, then, as if a dam had been unleashed, the entire crew poured down the ramp and disappeared into the crowd.

For a moment I feared I'd be swept away with them, but Toraan's tail snaked around my waist again, holding me steady amid the chaos and jubilation. When I looked up, the old Raas was staring at me.

His gaze drifted to Toraan's tail then back up to my face. "You are human."

I inclined my head to him as a show of respect. "I am."

"This is Rachael from the planet Horl," Toraan said. "She was a Zagrath admiral's intended bride."

Raas Maassen's pupils flared as he looked at Toraan. "You took her as your hostage?"

Toraan didn't look away, but he twitched. "Not as my hostage. As my mate."

There was no reply as the old Vandar slid his gaze back to me and then to Toraan. "You will explain to me?"

Toraan tapped his heels again. "Of course, uncle. I had hoped we could have a private audience before the banquet. There is much I need to tell you."

"I can see that." He spun on his heel, waving his nephew forward. "Come with me. Some of your raiders will be busy reuniting with their families, while the others will be toasted in the drinking hall while my staff prepares for the celebration. We will have time to confer."

The crowd flowed away from the ships and toward a sea of high-peaked tents. I followed behind Toraan, until he reached for my hand and pulled me forward to walk beside him. Even though he released my hand again, his touch sent warmth up my arm and calmed the fluttering in my stomach.

As we approached the tents, I realized they were not tents. At least, not any tent I'd ever seen. Although the roofs appeared to made of colorful fabric that rose high into the air and created a gigantic patchwork quilt of sorts, they sat atop actual buildings made of beige stone. Some of the buildings rose several stories into the air, and boasted balconies and terraces.

Toraan had told me that his people had originally been nomadic, living in tents on their home world of Vandar and roving the land in hordes. They'd taken the horde tradition to space, roving in warbirds, instead of on the backs of galloping beasts, and it seemed they echoed the nomadic tents of their ancestors in their colonies.

We walked down wide streets toward a tall building with a series of shiny spires that looked like they might be forged out of iron. Vandar peered down from balconies, their cheers morphing to curious glances when they spotted me.

Toraan seemed unconcerned by the curious attention, although he paused after we'd passed through the massive, wooden doors leading into what looked to me like a palace. "I would like Rachael to be fitted for a dress for the banquet."

Raas Maassen paused, his gaze flitting to me. "The horde is no longer equipped for a female, I see."

Toraan's cheeks flushed. "No. It is not."

The old Raas grunted, then waved a hand and another Vandar appeared by his side. "The human needs a new wardrobe fitting the mate of a Vandar. Take her and see to it."

The attendant—who could not have been more than a teenager, but still wore a leather kilt and had a massive, bare chest—clicked his heels and jerked his head to me.

I did not want to appear fearful, but was I supposed to follow a total stranger on a completely foreign planet and leave the one person I trusted? Before I could open my mouth, Toraan rested a hand on the small of my back.

"Go with him. I will find you later."

His uncle's gaze was on me, and I did not want to make Toraan look bad. I nodded without speaking, moving off with the Vandar attendant as Toraan and his uncle walked up one side of a sweeping, double staircase. Instead of going up the other side, I followed the Vandar through a massive hall, with high windows streaming light from all sides. Tables lined it from one end to the other, and it was clearly being set for the festivities. Without a backward glance, the Vandar led me through the hall and then down winding corridors until we reached a room lined with bolts of fabric covering the walls. As we entered, a female Vandar stood.

"Who have you brought me?"

"The new mate of Raas Toraan."

Her heavily-lined face registered a moment of shock before she rubbed her hands together. "Then we have our work cut out for us, don't we, dear?"

I tried to return her smile. The last dress fitting I'd had ended up with me running out, sneaking off a ship, escaping from the empire, and then getting captured by a Vandar warlord. I hoped this one would be a little less dramatic.

CHAPTER 30

Toraan

My uncle did not lead me to his personal chambers as I expected, but instead to a long, stone balcony on the top of the feasting hall. One side overlooking the expansive central hall, and the other overlooked the colony. Metal spires rose around us, creating a sensation of being surrounded by spikes.

He walked to the stone railing and peered out over the tented tops of the lower buildings. "I know these tents are what our forefathers would have seen as they walked among their hordes, but staying on land still feels unnatural to me."

I smiled, understanding him completely. "You miss raiding."

He twitched one shoulder. "I miss flying with the horde. No one tells you that you will miss the echo of steel as you walk, or the lurch as your warbird accelerates." He gave himself a small shake. "But I know the horde is in good hands with you. I have no regrets. It was time."

"I strive to live up to your reputation, Raas Maassen."

He smiled at me. "You are making your own name, as you should. You have always been your own warrior. So unlike your father and brother."

I knew this was a high compliment from my uncle, but I also knew that many considered my father and older brothers to be great Raas'. Violent and impulsive, perhaps, but no one could argue their damage to the empire. I myself heard of their victories, and sometimes doubted my more measured strategy.

"You are probably wondering why I have brought a human female with me," I said, beating him to the punch.

"Toraan." My uncle put a hand on my shoulder for a moment. "I never wonder about your actions. There is nothing you do that does not have a purpose. Nothing that does not play a part in a larger plan."

Expressed like that it sounded calculating and cold, but it had been how he'd trained me, so he did not mean to voice disapproval.

"As I mentioned, the female escaped from a Zagrath ship. She was intended as an imperial admiral's bride."

My uncle's brow quirked up. "I take it she did not find this admiral to her liking?"

"He is old and repulsive," I said. "According to her."

"And how did you come upon this escape artist?"

I turned to look out over the colony, resting my arms on the stone rail. "We responded to a call from Kaalek's horde. When we arrived, Kaalek and Kratos were in the process of running the empire off a planet."

"You saw your brothers?"

I shook my head without looking at him. "We'd maintained invisibility for a tactical advantage and were preparing to attack an imperial battleship when we saw the transport slipping away from it. The actions were subversive, so we followed."

My uncle let out a chuckle. "You always did love a good hunt or solving a puzzle."

"We waited until we were sure it was an escape, then we immobilized the ship and took it onboard."

"You thought it was a Zagrath traitor?"

Nodding, I glanced up at him. "It made sense that one of their fighters had gone rogue. We thought we'd nabbed a prisoner who could give us information about the enemy."

"And instead, you got a human bride."

"In a wedding gown."

My uncle let out a throaty laugh. "What I would have given to have seen your face."

Since I'd been starstruck when I'd first seen Rachael, I doubt my slack-jawed expression is what he would have expected.

"I take it you soon found a way to turn the situation to your advantage, like I taught you?"

My heart beat faster at the memory. "I made a deal with her. She needed protection from the empire, and she was willing to tell me what she knew about them in exchange for keeping her out of the admiral's clutches."

"A smart deal to make. Keeping a human on board is a small price to pay for Zagrath secrets."

"That is what I thought." Clouds moved over the sun, blocking the warmth of the rays for a moment.

"If the secrets were genuine," he added.

"I believe they are." I straightened. "According to the conversations she overheard from the admiral and his officers, they know of the existence of our colonies."

My uncle went still. "They know of Zendaren and the others? We have kept the locations secret for millennia."

"They are certain they exist—and I do not know how—but they have no knowledge of the locations."

Raas Maassen blew out a breath, his shoulders sagging. "Are they searching for us?"

I bit my lower lip. "This admiral seems determined to find Vandar colonies and destroy them."

My uncle's brow furrowed. "What is his name, this admiral who hates us so?"

"Admiral Kurmog."

The old Raas clutched the railing, his knuckles going white. "Kurmog." He said the name like a curse.

"You know him?" I had not personally encountered an imperial admiral named Kurmog, nor was I aware we'd raided any of his ships when I was apprenticing under my uncle, or after I'd taken control of the horde.

He pressed his lips together into a hard line before expelling a hiss of breath. "Long before you joined me on my warbird. It was one of the reasons your father and I became estranged."

I was quiet so he could continue. Although it had been no secret that my father and uncle—two of the Vandar's most notable Raas'—had stopped speaking before I was born, I had never had the temerity to ask why.

"Your father and I were not always at each other's throats. Even though we were very different warriors, when we were younger, we would often fly and raid together. Our hordes were like one."

I had never heard this. It was hard to imagine a time when my uncle and father were not bitter foes.

"We were liberating an alien planet together. The imperial ships had been able to harvest some of the planet's technology, so I wanted to board the lead ship and take it, while your father insisted we blow it from the sky. Our argument distracted us from the battle and the enemy ship with the technology managed to get away. Your father was so enraged he blew up every remaining enemy ship, taking out some of the forces from the alien planet in the process."

I drew in a breath. "He destroyed those we were trying to free?"

"It was not his intention, but yes." My uncle's face was twisted with regret. "I was livid and accused him of being reckless and dangerous and not fit to be Raas. He claimed that it was my inability to make the hard decisions that had caused the Zagrath to get away with the valuable technology. We were both right, but we were also responsible for many innocent deaths."

"I have never heard this."

The old Raas looked even older than his years as he rubbed a palm over his forehead. "It was not a point of pride for us. The planet we were liberating blamed us for the death of their people and the destruction of their air defenses. They refused any more of our help, and ended up accepting imperial rule."

Although this had happened before my tenure as a raider, I still felt ill at the thought. "And Kurmog?"

"The name of the remaining captain of the alien air defenses. The one who told us to leave their planet and welcomed the empire."

I let what he'd told me sink in, but it was almost hard to believe. "It appears he has not gotten over it—and now he's a Zagrath admiral."

"And now the Vandar have taken his bride."

I cursed to myself then out loud. "*Vrak*. I knew none of this when I decided to humiliate him."

My uncle shook his head slowly. "It does not matter. His hate for the Vandar has been festering for half a lifetime. You did not bring it upon us."

No, I thought. My father did.

"He will never forgive the female for running from him and into the arms of the Vandar. I hope you are prepared to offer her permanent protection. Or is that why you are here? Are you leaving her with us?"

"I have no intention of leaving her. As I said before, I've taken her as my mate."

"As part of your deal to protect her, yes? Giving her the designation as the mate of a Raas to ensure the Vandar will guard her with our lives."

"That was my original intent, but now I wish to give her more than that," I told him. "I wish to give her the protection of my mating marks."

CHAPTER 31

Toraan

Raas Maassen held my gaze, his own somber. "Mating marks are not something you can choose to give, nephew."

Now that I was Raas, my uncle never referred to me as his nephew anymore, but he was clearly making a point. I shifted under his scrutiny. "I understand the way our mating marks work."

"Then you know it is pointless to hope for them, unless she is your one true mate. Besides, she is not Vandar."

I drew in a breath as the clouds shifted to reveal the sun, and the warm beams returned to my face. "She would not be the first human to get mating marks. Kratos and his human bride share them."

Shock crossed my uncle's face. "Your eldest brother took a mate? A human mate?" He shook his head. "Impossible. He is still leading his horde as Raas."

We maintained a strict policy of non-communication with our colonies. It prevented the enemy from intercepting transmissions, and tracking their origination points.

"I assure you, it is possible." Although I had not seen the mating marks on my brother or his human mate, it had been confirmed by his *majak* in communication with mine. Besides, salacious news like that had spread through the hordes like wildfire. "He took a human female as a prisoner, and they formed enough of a bond that she took his marks. She now travels with him aboard his warbird. I hear that she dresses like a Vandar raider."

"Kratos?" Disbelief tinged his voice. He did not know my brothers like he knew me, but he knew enough of them to know they were not the type of raiders to go against Vandar tradition lightly.

"Rumor has it that Kaalek also has a human female on his ship, but I do not know if she is his mate, or if they share mating marks."

The old Raas staggered back, catching himself with one hand on the railing. "How can it be that half of the warriors leading our hordes are involved with human females?"

"They are humans, not Zagrath." It was a subtle distinction, but a crucial one. "And my female was running from the enemy."

My uncle grunted an acknowledgment of this. "You cannot shield her from the empire without taking her as your mate?"

"If she is mated to a Raas, she will have the protection and firepower of every Vandar to defend her."

His gaze searched my face. "That is the only reason?"

I didn't want to admit that what had started out as a strategic deal had become something else for me. I couldn't admit that Rachael was more to me than a way to strike a blow to the empire, not without admitting that being with her had opened my heart and made me feel again. My emotions were too fresh and too fragile, and I barely understood them myself. Besides, I didn't know if Rachael felt the same way.

She enjoyed my attentions, but I could not be certain that her moans and cries of pleasure were not the natural reactions of a female who had never been allowed much sexual pleasure. I'd certainly helped release her from her cocoon, but I didn't know if her feelings for me went beyond our physical connection. A little voice reminded me that if she did feel something deeper, she would be wearing my marks already.

"Toraan?" My uncle studied me, no doubt reading my conflicted emotions.

"Even if she does not take my marks, I have sworn to protect her and take her as my mate."

"Even if it means your heart will be broken again?"

His sharp words were a stinging reminder that I had been rejected before. I tightened my hands into fists. "This is not the same. Rachael will keep her end of the bargain."

The old Raas put his hands on my shoulders, his touch instantly diffusing my defensiveness. "You deserve more than a female who is bound to you out of obligation. I know I taught you that strategy is the most important skill a Raas can have, but strategy does not work when it comes to the heart. You cannot make a deal to find your one true mate."

"I never thought I would find my true mate. I gave up on that dream long ago."

My uncle squeezed my arms. "Vandar warriors never give up."

"Then I am not giving up on Rachael."

He pressed his lips together and dropped his hands. "Then it is done." He turned on his heel. "I need to confer with our security officers. The Zagrath might not have found us, but their search makes us more vulnerable." He glanced at me over his shoulder before leaving the balcony. "I am grateful to you for bringing this news to us, and I am glad to see you again, Toraan."

I watched him go, but did not follow. Instead, I turned and looked out over the colorful, fabric peaks of the colony. Streets wound between the houses in a meandering pattern, broken up with flowering patches of green. Beyond the tented houses stretched fields of gold—grain that would be harvested to feed the residents—and animals grazing on tightly-cropped grass. I imagined this was what the home world of Vandar had looked like before we'd been forced off it centuries before. But then, our hordes had not used stone to make buildings permanent or technology to fly through the skies. I wondered sometimes if our progress had all been good.

As I allowed the scenery to soothe me, doubt crept into my mind. As much as it frustrated me to have my uncle question my strategy and my intent, I knew he was right. I could not force mating marks, and so far it looked like that part of my plan was a failure. I flinched at this. I despised failure. I'd always believed deep in my soul that if I planned well enough and worked diligently, I would not fail. But I was failing at this, and there was nothing I could do about it.

I could not make Rachael love me, even if I loved her.

I jerked back, startled by the realization. Was it possible that I loved her? I frowned. Even though I'd spent most of the journey to Zendaren with my cock buried inside her, I had not expected my desire to grow into something deeper. She'd been a mission, but now I couldn't imagine my life without her.

"It doesn't matter," I muttered to myself. The lack of black marks curling across her skin were proof that she did not share my feelings. At that moment, I despised being a Vandar and having such an outward display of devotion. Could I stomach the humiliation of taking a mate who did not wear my marks—ever? I swallowed down the ache in my gut, reminding myself that I still claimed her as a mate. I'd made a promise.

I closed my eyes and groaned.

"It can't be that bad, Toraan."

The sultry, female voice from behind me made my eyes pop open. It had been a long time, but I could never forget that voice. "Lila." I did not turn, but braced my arms wide on the stone railing.

She laughed, the sound throaty. "You can't look at me?"

I gritted my teeth and turned. She was just as I remembered her—tall and beautiful with jet-black hair she wore in a high bun that contrasted with her alabaster skin. Long lashes fluttered as she curved her red lips into a seductive smile I'd seen many times before. "What are you doing here?"

"Looking for you, of course." She joined me at the overlook, her tail moving as languidly as she did. "I've been waiting for you to return."

I folded my arms over my chest. I did not have to look down at her, but I narrowed my gaze. "You rejected me and took another mate."

Something flickered behind her eyes, but her smile didn't falter. "I was young and impatient. I should have waited for you."

"You mean you should have waited for me to be named Raas."

"Toraan." She placed one slender hand on my chest and leaned into me. "Do you really think so little of me?"

"I think you got bored of waiting and took a raider who would warm your bed."

Lila pulled her hand back as if she'd been burned. "I did not know when you would return. Every other female was taking a mate."

Even though she was beautiful, she no longer stirred my desire. I saw nothing but cold calculation, and part of me wondered how I'd ever been so enamored of her. The smile I'd once found enchanting looked hard and brittle, and her seductive touch now felt practiced.

"I no longer blame you," I said. "But I also have nothing to say to you."

"You don't mean that." Her voice cracked even as her tail swished behind her.

I took a step back. "Why are you here, Lila?"

She released a breath and her smile vanished. She tugged at the neckline of her gown. "Because of this." There was nothing but creamy skin from her throat to the swell of her breasts. "I still don't have mating marks."

Her revelation was startling. I'd assumed she had taken her mate because they'd formed marks with each other. It had never occurred to me that she'd still be lacking in marks after so long. Without marks, there could be no offspring.

"Don't you see?" She released her grip on her dress and the fabric returned to cover her chest. "I made a horrible mistake that affected both of us. We're supposed to be together. It was always supposed to be you and me. That's why neither of us have marks."

I stared at her, taking in what she'd said. I refused to believe that the female who'd broken my heart was my one true mate. But what she'd said was true. Neither of us had formed mating marks with another, and obviously not for lack of trying.

"It does not matter," I managed to say. "We both have mates."

"Mates we will never share marks with." Her tone was bitter even as her tail curled around my leg. "We will never have children or a legacy. Is that really what you want?"

My mind swirled with conflicting thoughts, but I shook my head and flickered her tail away with my own. "It does not matter. It is done."

Lila's smile returned as she backed away from me. "What is done can be undone."

CHAPTER 32

Rachael

"I should wait for Toraan." I stopped at the door to the large hall, wiping my palms down the soft fabric of my new dress, then instantly regretting it.

I didn't need to worry. The seamstress wasn't paying attention to me. Her eyes were on the boisterous crowd filling the long, feasting hall, even as one hand was on my back, prodding me forward.

"My instructions were to deliver you to the dais. The Raas will join you there." She huffed out a breath. "*Vaes.*"

I scanned the expansive space for Toraan, but couldn't spot him anywhere. It wasn't an easy feat to pick him out of the crowd, since all the Vandar had dark hair and wore battle kilts. All the males, that was. The female Vandar were split into two camps—

some were dressed in kilts and armor like the raiders, and others wore dresses that draped long over their legs.

The Vandar seamstress who'd been tasked with dressing me for the occasion had gone with the latter option, creating a simple dress out of a shimmery, gold fabric that hung from one shoulder, gathered at my waist, and cascaded to the floor. Although my arms were bare, my legs were completely covered.

She seemed proud of her creation, although I got the feeling she wasn't thrilled I was human. She'd made more than a few disapproving noises as she'd fitted me, especially when she'd realized I had no tail.

"The banquet is a great honor," the old woman said, as she attempted to move me through the tall, arched doorway. "And everyone wants to see the human Toraan brought back from his raiding campaign."

That's what I was afraid of. I might have been trained in protocol, but that didn't mean I relished the thought of being stared at by hundreds of aliens. Aliens who were known throughout the galaxy for being ruthless. Even though Toraan was not the bloodthirsty raider I'd been expecting, how could I be sure the others weren't? Still, I didn't have a choice.

I snaked through the crowd toward the front, attracting surprised glances and causing a wave of whispers to trail behind me. When we reached the raised platform lined with high-backed chairs and a single, long table, I let out a sigh of relief.

Toraan stood next to one of the chairs, talking to another raider. I fought the urge to call out his name, but I was glad when he spotted me.

He waved me forward, and met me at the top of the short flight of steps, his gaze taking in my dress. "The dressmaker did a good job."

I turned to introduce the woman, but she was gone. I turned back to the Raas, leaning into him. "I'm glad you're here. I was starting to feel out of place."

"You have nothing to fear," he told me as he led me to a chair behind the table and pulled it out. "This is a celebration."

I nodded, but I couldn't help noticing that his jaw was tight. Toraan did not look like he was enjoying himself, either.

He took the seat next to me, but was immediately pulled into a conversation with the Vandar on his other side. I took the opportunity to look out over the crowd. Guests were still pouring in and filling the hall, bodies jostling each other for places at the tables. Light no longer streamed in from the high windows, but candles burned in sconces on the walls and down the tables, as servers filled goblets and deposited trays laden with food.

On the warbird, I'd gotten used to Vandar food—at least what the raiders ate—but I recognized little of what was on the trays placed in front of me. A rich, savory scent wafted up from some kind of grilled meat, and the aroma of bread was familiar.

The more people that filled the hall, the louder the buzz of voices and bursts of laughter. Raiders slammed goblets back down on the tables and pounded their fists, and even Toraan laughed next to me.

I took a gulp of wine and peered over him. He was seated next to his uncle, the old Raas who had greeted us at the ship and had seemed less than pleased to learn about me. I suspected he and

Toraan had talked, and he now knew about the deal I'd made, but still, he eyed me with suspicion.

"You should eat." Toraan motioned to my empty plate, before turning back to his conversation with his uncle.

I'd been expecting some sort of welcome or blessing of the food, but it seemed that was not part of Vandar tradition. As I'd learned on the warbird, the Vandar did not use utensils, so I gingerly pulled several morsels of grilled meat onto my plate using a wedge of flatbread.

"That is better when eaten with these." Toraan's *majak*, who was seated next to me and had been talking to the warrior on his other side until that moment, handed me a small basket of brown rolls.

I blinked at him for a few moments. I didn't think the raider had ever said more than a few words to me before, and I'd always gotten the idea that he disapproved of my presence on the raiding ship. "Thank you."

He grunted and gave a half shrug, gesturing with his head to the raucous crowd. "This must be overwhelming for you."

"I think there are more people in this one room than in my entire town on Horl," I admitted, taking the basket from him.

"A gathering this large is not an everyday occurrence for us either. But the return of a horde is always something to be celebrated, since it does not happen often."

"Do you miss this when you're in space?" I asked. "Your families and female Vandar, I mean."

A smile teased his mouth. "You are aware that we do not deprive ourselves of female company while on raiding campaigns."

My cheeks warmed. "Your families, then."

"It is a sacrifice worth making." He looked out over the crowd again. "But it is always good to come home, even for those of us who have families on other colonies."

I bit into a roll as he turned back to the raider on his other side. I'd never imagined I would be visiting a planet so far from my own, much less a secret colony of the elusive Vandar. Then again, my life had taken an unexpected turn when Toraan's ship had captured me.

I glanced over at the Raas and caught him looking at me, his expression somber. Before I could ask him if he was okay, his uncle stood and raised his glass.

"Tonight, we welcome back Raas Toraan and his crew of valiant raiders. They bring us tales of bloody battles, imperial ships destroyed, and planets liberated. We raise our glasses to their bravery and valor, and the honor they bring to Lokken and the gods of old."

Cheers rose up throughout the hall as goblets were raised. "To Lokken!"

I drank along with everyone else, the strong wine buzzing my fingertips almost immediately.

Then Toraan stood, greeting his kinsman and raising his goblet to first his uncle and then to his crew. Again, we all drank as attendants hurried to refill glasses.

As I nibbled on a roll to keep from getting too drunk, I noticed a female at the front of the crowd. She was strikingly beautiful and held herself as if she was fully aware of it. She was also staring unabashedly at Toraan.

I wanted to ask him who she was and why she was looking at him like she wanted to eat him, but he was continuing to toast his command deck warriors. I took another drink, and told myself that she must be a member of his family, happy to have him home.

When I heard my name, my attention snapped to Toraan.

"It is appropriate that I introduce her for the first time to you, my fellow raiders, family, and friends." He looked down at me, placing a hand on my shoulder. "I have taken her as my mate and my Raisa."

The laughter and talking ceased as all eyes swiveled to me. I tried to smile, but my face burned, and my cheeks quivered. The Vandar were not cheering and drinking to me. They were shocked by his announcement, and not at all pleased.

I summoned every ounce of duty drilled into me by my mother, and I straightened my shoulders and looked out over the heads that were now facing me. I would not let myself look weak, even if I had to dig my fingernails into my own arm to keep from crying.

Before the silence could stretch out any longer, the old Raas rose from his seat. "To Raas Toraan and his Raisa."

"To Raas Toraan and his Raisa," the crowd echoed, then there were a few cheers, and finally, the hall erupted in thumping and hooting.

Toraan sat, reaching over and squeezing my hand briefly. I allowed my shoulders to slump, then I caught the regal Vandar female staring again. But this time, it was not the Raas who'd captured her attention. It was me. Or, more specifically, my neckline. Her gaze was locked onto the unmarked skin exposed by my one-shouldered gown. Then she looked up at me and smiled.

CHAPTER 33

Rachael

I swallowed hard, the sweetness of the wine churning in my stomach. Even though the female smiled, her eyes were cold as they met mine. I forced myself to look away, and when I gathered the courage to glance back, she'd gone.

Although it probably wasn't a great idea, I took another gulp of wine, my hand trembling as I held the goblet. When I'd drained it, I felt a little better. At least, I felt numb.

You're imagining things, I told myself. *She wasn't anything more than a curious Vandar who'd never seen a human before.*

Unlike the raiders who flew around the galaxy interacting with all kinds of aliens, the Vandar who lived on the colony were isolated. Unless the raiders brought visitors regularly—which I knew they didn't, from the startled reactions I'd been getting—

none of the residents had ever laid eyes on anyone who didn't look exactly like them.

"Kind of like me before I left Horl," I whispered to myself. Although I'd seen imperial officers and soldiers because they occupied our planet, other aliens had not been a common sight.

"Have you had enough to eat?" Toraan asked me, lowering his head to my ear to be heard above the din.

I nodded, even though I'd barely done more than nibble on a piece of bread. "Did you notice the female in the front who was staring at you?"

Toraan patted my hand, although his face contorted for a moment. "We are the guests of honor. Everyone is looking at us."

He was right. I must have imagined the female's intensity. I eyed my empty goblet. No more wine for me.

My stomach no longer churned, but my head swam as I sat on the dais, watching the Vandar drink and eat. It didn't help that the heat from the bodies and the burning candles had made the cavernous hall steamy. I fanned myself with one hand, glad my dress was sleeveless, but wishing the fabric didn't cover my legs and pool around my feet.

A steady stream of warriors came onto the dais to talk to Toraan, and I saw that his plate was as untouched as mine. Shouts and bellowing laughter rose up, and scuffles broke out but dissolved into more laughter. Compared to the staid meals I'd been used to on Horl, this was more like dinner and a brawl.

I waited for an appropriate time to interrupt Toraan, but I finally turned to Rolan. "Where are the…?" I didn't know the polite term for bathroom—if the Vandar even had one—but I suspected that asking him for the powdering chamber would only confuse him.

His brow wrinkled for a moment before a look of awareness crossed his face. He jerked his head back and to one side. "Behind the hall. Would you like me to escort you?"

I stood, bracing the tips of my fingers on the table for balance. "No, thank you. I'm sure I can manage."

I almost groaned at myself. Ugh. I sounded so much like my mother when I parroted the polite phrases she'd drilled into me.

Toraan's first officer inclined his head at me, standing briefly as I did and allowing me to pass him. Holding the fabric of my dress with one hand so I wouldn't trip on it, I slowly descended the short staircase. Luckily, there was so much noise and chaos, my departure wasn't noticed, and I weaved my way through the crush of people and out an arched doorway to one side of the dais.

As soon as I was out of the hall, the noise diminished, and the air was not so stifling. I put a hand to the stone wall, savoring the coolness as I closed my eyes. A wave of dizziness washed over me, and I sucked in a breath.

"Are you unwell, dear?"

I pressed my lips together, tasting bile in the back of my throat, but I didn't open my eyes. "I'm fine, thank you."

A hand circled my waist. "You should rest. It seems the Vandar wine was too much for you."

I bristled at the suggestion that I was drunk, even though the floor felt like it was shifting under my feet. I was too unsteady to resist being led to a hard seat, and when I opened my eyes I was sitting on a bench.

"That *is* better," I admitted, already regaining my equilibrium. I glanced at the person sitting beside me and reared back.

It was the female who'd been staring at Toraan and then at me. "You."

She didn't appear ruffled by me recoiling. "Oh? Has he told you about me?"

The Vandar female was even more striking up close than she was from a distance, her statuesque figure so perfect and her skin so creamy she appeared to have been carved from marble. Next to her, I felt like a child.

Finally, her words permeated my muddled brain. "Has who told me about you?"

Her lips curved into a pitying smile. "Toraan. If you know who I am, he must have told you about us."

What was she talking about? "Are you family?"

She let out a peal of laughter that echoed off the tall stone walls of the corridor. "I'm Lila."

Was that supposed to mean anything to me? I took in her imperious smile and folded my arms over my chest. This female was starting to get on my nerves. "I'm sorry, but I've never heard that name—from Toraan, or any of the other Vandar."

She smiled again, but her jaw was tight. "I can see why he'd want to keep me a secret, although it doesn't seem fair to you."

I didn't reply, but narrowed my gaze at her.

"I know about your deal." She'd dropped her voice to a whisper. "I heard Toraan telling his uncle all about it."

That gave me pause, but then why shouldn't Toraan tell his uncle? We'd come here so he could warn them about the empire, and I was the reason the Vandar now knew that Admiral Kurmog was searching for their colonies.

"I felt so sorry for you when I heard him say that you weren't really his mate," she continued with a sympathetic smile. "And that he's only using you to strike back at the Zagrath."

My first impulse was to snap back at her that it wasn't true, but hadn't that been our deal? To form a mating bond to keep me safe and humiliate the empire? "Maybe at first, but not anymore."

"No?" She arched her eyebrows. "Then where are your marks?"

My gaze dropped to my chest and the unmarked flesh peeking out from beneath the gold fabric. She was right. If Toraan and I were more to each other, wouldn't I have marks?

A cold realization settled over me. Unless only my feelings had changed. It didn't matter if I'd fallen hard for the Raas. If he didn't feel the same way, I'd never get his mating marks. A fresh wave of nausea made me press my fingers to my mouth.

"Toraan is too honorable to go back on his deal, but the Vandar will never accept a mate who does not share marks." Her whisper had become a hiss. "Is that what you want? You can never give him a family, and being with you will only weaken his standing as Raas. You will never be his Raisa. You will be his destruction."

I jerked away from her and stood, swaying on my feet. "Who are you?"

"I was meant to be his mate." Her smile had vanished, and her face was now twisted in anger. "I was his first love, and I still hold his heart."

As much as I wanted to denounce her as a liar, there was truth in her words. My stomach roiled and heat prickled my skin as I staggered away from her.

"You will never be his one true love."

Even though her final words were no more than a whisper, they reverberated off the walls and followed me as I hurried down the corridor, both hands pressed on the rough stone to keep myself from collapsing.

CHAPTER 34

Toraan

I sat back and swigged my wine, grateful for a break from the steady stream of Vandar who had monopolized my attention most of the evening. Glancing over to check on Rachael, I was startled to see an empty chair beside me.

Tvek. How long had she been gone?

Leaning over, I prodded my *majak's* arm. "Rolan, did you see my mate leave?"

He flicked his gaze to the empty chair between us. "She has not returned? She excused herself to the washing chamber, but I would have thought she'd be back by now."

I scanned the feasting hall, but did not see a flash of her gold dress. "Was she ill?"

He shook his head. "She did not look ill." He looked at her plate with cold food on it, and one half-eaten chunk of bread perched on the edge. "But she also did not eat much."

I lifted her goblet, swirling the few droplets at the bottom. "While finishing her wine."

I cursed myself for not paying better attention to her. I'd been so distracted by the Vandar who had wanted to greet me and hear about our latest campaign, many friends and family I had not seen in an age.

"That's no excuse," I muttered to myself as I stood, my heavy chair scraping the floor as I pushed it back. I'd neglected my mate for too long. Now I needed to find her and make amends. My heartbeat quickened as I thought about all the ways I could apologize to her, most of them involving her spread out naked beneath me.

"Do you wish me to join you?" Rolan asked, standing as well.

I clapped a hand on his arm. "No. Stay and enjoy the banquet." My gaze landed on Viken in the chair next to him with a female in his lap. "Like our battle chief."

Rolan rolled his eyes, but resumed his seat.

I strode off the dais and from the hall, walking purposefully toward the washing chambers. I hoped Rachael was not ill. Although she'd drunk Vandar wine before, it had been watered down to make our ship's supplies last longer. The wine on Zendaren was not.

The quiet of the corridors was a welcome respite from the bustling banquet, and I was grateful they were virtually empty. I passed a handful of raiders, who snapped their heels dutifully even though their eyes looked bleary, but there was no sign of Rachael.

When I reached the door to the female washing chamber, I poked my head inside and called her name. No response. I stepped in and made quick work of searching the round room, looking in every empty compartment.

Stepping back outside, I rubbed a hand across my forehead. Where could she have gone? Had she gotten lost in the corridors leading back to the feasting hall?

"There you are."

I turned at the voice even though it did not belong to Rachael. "Lila."

She glided toward me, her smile no less sultry and artificial than it had been earlier. "You don't sound pleased to see me, Toraan."

"We have already talked. What else is there to say?"

She tilted her head to one side. "I thought some good food and wine might soften you up and help you see clearly."

Although I had once believed her to be the most beautiful female in the universe, I now found her beauty cold and empty. "I see you clearly enough, Lila."

Her smile faltered for a moment, but she advanced on me, backing me almost to the wall and pressing her hands to my bare chest. "You know I'm right. We were meant to be together."

I put my hands on hers to push them away. "You have a mate, and so do I."

"But neither of us have mating marks. Don't you see what that means? We made a horrible mistake."

"We?" I let out a bitter laugh. "You took a mate while I was away on a raiding campaign. I fail to see how that is my mistake."

"Fine." She huffed out a breath. "I made a mistake, but you took a human for a mate just to punish the empire."

"That is not the only reason. She requested asylum, and I granted it."

"She will never wear your mating marks, Toraan." Her eyes blazed as she looked at me. "You know, I know it, everyone in the banquet hall knows it. You have been fucking her for the entire journey to Zendaren, and still she remains unmarked."

I flinched at her words. "How do you know that?"

She shrugged. "Did you expect it to be a secret from your crew? I have heard them talking about the human that has been keeping the Raas occupied in his chambers. I know you well enough to know what that means. Don't you remember when you used to be content to fuck me until I couldn't walk?"

Memories flooded my mind, but I forced them away. "I remember."

She rubbed her hands down my chest muscles and across the ridges of my stomach. "It can be like that again, Toraan." Her tail moved up my legs and under my kilt. "Let me show you everything I've learned since you've been gone."

I clenched my jaw and clutched her hands to keep them from slipping beneath the waistband of my kilt. I tried to step back, but the wall stopped me. "Lila."

"Let me give you what the human never can, Toraan." She peered up at me and licked her lips. "Mating marks and offspring. Vandar offspring, who can join you on your warbird and be your legacy. You know as well as I do that the human female can never provide you with either."

I gritted my teeth as the fur of her tail caressed my thigh, using my own tail to pull it away. I did not desire her, but I was only Vandar, and being stroked had made my cock twitch beneath my kilt.

Lila smiled, her gaze dropping to the bulge beneath my kilt. "See? I can still arouse you. Why are you fighting what we both know is right?"

I took her wrists in my hands and her pupils flared. "You wish to hold me down?"

I pushed her away from me, and she stumbled back. "I wish you to leave me alone."

She righted herself and rubbed her wrists. "You're being a fool."

"And you are making a fool of yourself, Lila. I have a mate, and even though she is a human, I love her."

Lila gaped at me. "You don't mean that. You can't possibly love that creature over me."

"I do." I shook my head at her. "I never loved you. What we had was childish infatuation, and I am grateful to you for betraying me and releasing me from any connection I might have felt for you."

It had taken a long time, but I no longer felt anything when I looked at her. Not pain, not hurt, and certainly not regret.

"You're making a mistake." Her words were no longer sultry, but biting and hard. "This will ruin you."

"I've never been more sure about anything in my life than I am about Rachael." I took a step toward her. "You are the one who should be worried that news of your disloyalty does not reach the ears of your mate. He serves in my eldest brother's horde, does he not?"

Her lovely features morphed into a mask of rage. "You will lose your mate before I lose mine, Toraan." She let out a chilling laugh. "You've already lost her, and you don't even know it."

My skin prickled as dread settled over me. "What does that mean?"

"It means that you should have told your human about me. She seemed genuinely surprised to know that you had a first love you'd never mentioned."

I advanced on her, pushing her up against the opposite wall. "What have you done?"

She smiled up at me, even as her eyes flashed dark and deadly. "Only the truth that you should have told her."

Fury bubbled up in my chest as I bit out my question. "Which is?"

"That if she never takes your marks, then you will never have children, or a legacy, and she will never actually be your Raisa, no matter how many times you say the word." When she'd finished spitting out the words, her chest was heaving.

I released her and backed away, the blood pounding in my ear. "Go," I whispered. When she didn't move, I advanced on her with my hands in tight fists. "Go!"

She jumped and scurried away, finally leaving me alone in the corridor. I bent over and sucked in air, trying to calm the fury that threatened to overwhelm me. I wasn't angry at Lila, even though I would have enjoyed wringing her neck.

No, I was furious at myself. I hadn't been honest with Rachael about my past, or about what I felt for her. And now she'd had her mind poisoned by Lila. What must she think of me?

I straightened and took a long breath. It was done, and it could not to be undone. Now, I needed to find Rachael and beg her to forgive me.

CHAPTER 35

Rachael

I held a hand over my mouth, trying to keep from crying out as I watched Lila run her hands over Toraan, and slip her tail up under his kilt. Hearing her remind Toraan that I had not taken his mating marks and would never be able to give him what she could had been bad enough, but watching her touch him was too much.

I pulled my head from around the corner, hating the fact that I'd stumbled upon the two of them. I'd intended to announce myself, but that was before I'd heard her talk about fucking him. Part of me hadn't believed her when she insisted she'd been his first love, but Toraan hadn't denied a word she'd said.

"I remember." The deep husk of his voice in reply had made my stomach lurch.

I shook my head as I hurried away from them. I didn't want to listen to another word or, even worse, watch her do more than touch him.

This had been a mistake. Coming to the Vandar colony, agreeing to the deal with Raas Toraan, thinking I could consent to be his mate without falling for him. A huge, horrible mistake.

He was a badass warlord of the Vandar, who'd had more lovers than I could probably count and had never promised me anything but protection from the empire. It wasn't his fault I'd fallen for him, but I also couldn't stick around now that I knew he didn't feel the same way.

I choked back a sob. He deserved to be with someone who wouldn't hold him back, and it was clear that I wasn't that person. I glanced down at my chest. I couldn't even get his mating marks, and I'd spent most of the past few days with him fucking me senseless.

I paused and peered around. I'd been stumbling along without paying attention to where I was going, and now I was lost.

"Just great," I said under my breath. I wasn't sure where I wanted to go, but as far away from Lila and Toraan sounded like a good start. The noise of the banquet had vanished, so I guessed I was going in the opposite direction, and after taking a few more turns, I spotted a tall door.

Pushing it open, I found myself outside the building in some sort of alley. I sucked in a deep breath, glad for the cold, night air, even though I shivered and rubbed my bare arms. It took me a few moments to get my bearings, but I soon realized I was behind the banqueting hall. All I had to do was follow the walls around to the front, and I'd be able to retrace my steps to the warbird. I remembered the exact route we'd taken when we arrived, and was grateful once more for excellent recall.

"Vaes," I told myself as I started walking, the Vandar command urging me on.

I edged around the massive building until I reached the front then turned in the direction of the shipyard and away from the revelry. It might not have been my home, but the ship was the last place I'd been content. Right now, all I wanted to do was go back to the Raas' quarters, rip off my dress, sink into the bathing pools, and forget everything that had happened.

Luckily, everyone in the colony appeared to be at the celebration. Though laughter and shouting spilled from the doors of the feasting hall, the streets were empty as I hurried through them. I grabbed fistfuls of my dress and hiked it up, breaking into a run to combat the cold that made my teeth chatter. Soon, I spotted the wide-open expanse of the shipyard, and the hulking hulls of the Vandar ships, perched on the ground with their massive wings outstretched like a flock of birds about to take off.

I heaved out a grateful breath but didn't slow my pace. There were no guards at the entrance ramp of Toraan's lead ship, so I ran up and inside. The ship was eerily quiet. The engines didn't rumble, and heavy footsteps didn't rattle the staircases. It was like stepping onto a ghost ship, which was what many thought of the Vandar anyway.

I knew my way to the Raas's quarters, but my feet wouldn't take me. I stood rooted to the spot, thinking how different the ship felt without its crew—and without him. Then it hit me that it would never feel the same. He would never feel the same, not after what I'd heard and what I knew. I couldn't roll back time and pretend not to know, as much as I wished I could.

The time I'd spent with the Raas had been like a magical interlude, but it hadn't been real. We had never been real. We'd been a military strategy that, for a while, had felt like something more than that. But it hadn't been for him. It had always been a deal. His heart had never been mine, even though I knew mine had belonged to him for a while.

I bit the inside of my mouth to keep from crying, but tears clouded my vision. I wanted to run, just like I'd run from Kurmog. But there was nowhere to run but back to the colony, and that was the last place I wanted to be. No, I needed to get far away. If I left Toraan—truly left him—he'd no longer feel bound to the deal he'd made me. He could pick a Vandar female who could give him everything I couldn't.

The thought of never seeing him again made the tears spill from my eyes and trickle down my cheeks. I swiped at them furiously. It was better than being with someone who didn't return your love.

Once I knew what I had to do, I strode through the ship, quickly locating the hangar bay, and finding the Zagrath ship I'd arrived on. It was just as I'd left it, and the sight of the transport brought back all the feelings that I'd had when I'd snuck on it in the first place. It was hard to believe everything that had happened since I'd last been inside it, and it was just as painful to be sneaking back on it to run away.

"This is different," I said as I opened the ramp and walked up. "This will be better for everyone."

I sat in the cockpit, running my fingers over the console. I might not have been trained to fly, but I'd used my memory of the imperial pilot's movements when I'd been transported from Horl and now I would use that same perfect recall to help me escape again. I pressed the button to raise the entrance ramp and fired up the engines. The ship rumbled to life, lights illuminating the inside of the ship.

I hesitated, half expecting raiders to come running, but no one appeared. I held the control column as I lifted the ship off the floor of the hangar bay, careful to hold it steady as I maneuvered around the other ships. When it was in position, I engaged the thrusters and rocketed out of the warbird, pulling back hard to fly straight up. The ship trembled as it flew higher, but it shot through the planet's cloud cover and then out of the atmosphere and into space.

I leveled the ship, making sure not to look back as I flew away from Zendaren and Raas Toraan. "It is done."

CHAPTER 36

Toraan

When I entered the feasting hall, the crowd had thinned out and the din was now only a low buzz. Heads were slumped on tables and candles had dripped to nubs, the light flickering as platters were cleared. The warmth of the hall was made even more cloying by the scent of burning tallow and the pungent tang of spilled wine that was sticky on the floor.

It took me only a moment to scan the long room and see that Rachael had not returned. I'd already done a cursory search of the corridors around the hall and even returned to the washing chamber, startling a few females with my intrusion.

I leapt onto the dais without bothering with the stairs. Rolan and Viken looked up as the platform shook.

"What is it Raas?" Rolan asked, reacting first to my scowl.

"Rachael." I grasped the sides of my chair and looked out over the room. "I cannot find her."

Rolan put his goblet down on the table and stood. "She was not in the washing chamber?"

I shook my head. "I have searched everywhere."

"She must have gotten lost." Viken pushed the female off his lap and joined us in standing. "This building has many corridors."

"There is more." I didn't look either raider in the eyes. "She spoke to Lila."

"Lila?" Rolan recoiled at the name. "How?"

"She's been here watching you all night, Raas," Viken said. "I thought from the way she looked at you that you had an arrangement."

"An arrangement?" I gaped at my battle chief.

Viken's face reddened. "Like I said, she was obvious in her attentions. I could not have been the only one to notice it. Knowing your history, I thought…"

I recalled Rachael asking about a female staring at me. I'd dismissed her concerns as ridiculous—and then Lila had found her and told her everything. She must have thought I was purposefully misleading her. I clenched the sides of the chair until the bones of my knuckles were white against my skin.

"I have no arrangement with Lila," I said. "She wishes to resume things, but I do not. I told her as much when she confronted me."

"You rejected her." Rolan folded his arms over his chest. "And then she found your mate."

Viken frowned. "What did Lila tell the human?"

I gave my head a brusque shake. I didn't know what Lila had said, but I could guess. "Enough to make Rachael run."

Rolan squared his shoulders. "If she is not here, she might have returned to the ship."

"You think a human who has never set foot on Zendaren before could make her way through the colony and board our warbird?" Viken pressed his brows together as he spoke, clearly thinking the concept was far-fetched.

I thought about Rachael. She'd been brave enough to sneak off an imperial ship, steal a Zagrath transport ship, and fly away in the middle of a battle with two Vandar hordes. Making her way through a colony would not be nearly as scary. I allowed myself a breath. At least on Zendaren, she was not in danger.

"Rolan and I will return to the ship to see if what he surmises is true." I pivoted to Viken. "You will make another search of this building. She might still be here, somewhere."

Viken rapped his heels together. "Yes, Raas. We will find her."

Raas Maassen scraped his chair back and stood. "Who is missing?" His gaze went to the empty seat next to mine and he frowned. "Your human mate?"

"She went to the washing chamber and did not return." I attempted to make light of the situation. I did not want to give my uncle a reason to find fault with Rachael. "There is a high likelihood she got turned around in the maze of corridors."

The old Raas shifted his gaze to all three of us. "What are you not telling me?"

Rolan and Viken both cut their eyes to me, but remained silent. I'd forgotten that my uncle might be older than he had been when I had flown with him, but he was no less shrewd. There was no use in lying to the Vandar. He'd always been able to unravel my boyhood lies, and now I was a Raas. A Raas did not lie.

"She encountered Lila," I said.

Understanding passed across the elder's lined face. "That one should have been born a male. She is as ruthless as any raider, and twice as cunning."

His words shocked me. "You believe she would have made a good mate for a Raas?"

He moved his head slowly back and forth. "No. She would have made a decent Raas, but she is not the mate you need. You are all strategy and reason. You do not need a mate who is also calculating." He rested a hand on my arm. "You need a mate who can balance your logic and soften your measured mind. Just like the one you found."

"You approve of Rachael?" My voice was hoarse. "Even though she is human?"

His mouth twitched into a crooked smile. "Do not be so surprised. There is no great strategy without balance, and I have been watching. The human female gives you balance." His eyes clouded with grief for a moment. "My own Raisa was not who my father would have chosen. She did not come from a line of great warlords."

I remembered little of his Raisa, except that her death had devastated him. It had been another reason I had not been eager to find a mate. Before Rachael, my only experience with females had been that of loss.

"But what of the mating marks?" I asked. "What if it is not possible for her to get them?"

Raas Maassen shrugged. "It is not Vandar tradition, but it is possible. Do not your brothers have human mates who have taken their marks? If Kaalek with all his rash behavior can take a mate and share marks with her, there is no reason you cannot."

It was the same reasoning I'd used with myself, but I was startled to hear the argument from the old Raas. Especially since I'd been the one to tell him about Kratos and the marks he shared with his human. I narrowed my eyes at him. "Wait. How do you know that Kaalek's mate took his marks? I told you about Kratos, but even I have not even confirmed that Kaalek's human is marked. Neither horde has returned to Zendaren since they took their mates, have they?"

"They have not," my uncle said, without answering my other questions.

I fixed my gaze on my uncle. "Have you been in contact with my brothers?"

Before he could respond, a warrior rushed up to the dais. "Raas Maassen!"

My uncle turned at the urgent tone, instantly becoming the warlord I'd served under for so long. "Report."

The Vandar threw back his shoulders. "Planetary defenses report that a ship has left our atmosphere."

"A ship?" My uncle cocked his head. "A Vandar ship has departed without authorization?" He pivoted to me. "Do you know anything about one of your horde ships leaving?"

"No, Raas," the warrior said, pulling our attention back to him. "It is not a Vandar ship." He hesitated before speaking again, clearly conflicted and confused by the report he was giving. "It was a Zagrath ship."

My heart clenched, and I knew immediately who had flown away from Zendaren in an enemy ship.

CHAPTER 37

Rachael

I inhaled deeply, the spicy scent of the water tickling my nose. My head lolled back on the stone ledge as the water lapped around my neck, and I let out a sigh. Being back in the bathing pools felt right. Being back in the Raas' quarters felt right.

I sank deeper in the warm water, trying to ignore the beeping sound. What was that? Was someone trying to get in? Was Toraan getting a transmission? Come to think of it, where was Toraan?

The beeping became more shrill, and my eyes flew open. Damn. I wasn't in the bathing pools in Raas Toraan's quarters. I was sitting in the pilot's chair in the Zagrath transport I'd taken off the Vandar warbird.

Disappointment washed over me, but I shook it off. I'd left for a very good reason. There was no point in having second thoughts now, especially since I'd been flying for at least half an astro-cycle.

My gaze dropped to the console and to the flashing, red light. I wasn't an expert in navigation, but it appeared that I'd gone a little off course. The auto-pilot feature must have rerouted me around something while I was sleeping. I tapped the flat panel to reset the course, hesitating slightly.

I'd managed to set my end destination as Horl, even though I knew I couldn't return to my home planet without being turned over to the admiral again. The only problem was I didn't have anywhere else to go. I didn't *know* any other place to go.

"I'll figure something out before I get there," I said to myself, glad to hear my own voice break the silence.

But what? I'd been impulsive before, but I'd always had an excellent reason and a sense that there was something better out there. Now, I wasn't so sure. I'd found something better in Toraan, and I'd run from him. Did I really think I was going to find someone I felt the same way about, or even a place that would welcome me?

I peered out the glass at the blackness of space. Sitting alone in the cockpit, the reality of what I'd done sank in, along with a gnawing sense of regret. I'd been so sure when I'd taken the ship. So sure I was doing the right thing, but the truth was I'd been hurt. Hurt that Toraan hadn't told me about his past, and hurt that I couldn't give him what a Vandar female could.

"You didn't even give him a chance to explain," I whispered.

I pressed my lips together, the loneliness of space and the knowledge that I had nothing and no one to run to hitting me. What had I been thinking?

I sat up and narrowed my gaze at the navigational systems. I needed to turn this ship back around. I had to go back to Zendaren and talk to Toraan. I owed him that much.

Tapping at the console, I managed to reverse course, and the ship banked to one side. Even though the view hadn't changed much when I was flying in the opposite direction, I let out a breath knowing that I was flying toward Toraan.

When the transport jerked hard and I flew forward, the safety straps were the only things that kept me from hitting the floor. I looked down at the ship's readouts for an explanation, but I knew why I'd stopped.

My pulse fluttered wildly. Toraan had found me. He'd come after me.

The tug of my ship being pulled into another was familiar. The last time I'd been taken into the Vandar warbird, I'd been terrified. This time, I was elated.

I couldn't see much as the tractor beam drew me in from behind, but I leaned back and tried to calm myself. I didn't expect Toraan to be thrilled with me. I'd run from him, after all. I would have a lot of explaining to do. Then again, so would he.

But he'd come after me. That was all that mattered.

I unhooked myself from the chair and went to the door, bracing my hands on the walls to retain my balance as the ship entered the hangar bay.

"Play it cool," I told myself as the ship touched down, jostling me. Running down the ramp and throwing myself into his arms would not be good, even though that was exactly what I wanted to do.

I pressed the panel next to the ramp to lower it, bouncing on the balls of my feet as I waited for it to drop. When the steel hit the floor with a thud, my blood went cold.

Toraan was not at the bottom of the ramp waiting for me. No Vandar raiders were.

"How lucky we were to find you," Admiral Kurmog said as he stood with his hands clasped behind his back and his gaze locked on me. "We'd almost given up."

My knees nearly buckled, but I managed to stay standing. The Vandar had not come after me. The Zagrath had.

"I suggest you come out before I find it necessary to drag you off." The admiral's voice lost none of its smoothness as he threatened me.

I walked down the ramp with as much courage as I could muster, holding my head high and hoping my hands weren't shaking as badly as my legs were. The Zagrath I'd been promised to was just as bald and wrinkled as I remembered, his slate-blue uniform crisp, and his expression hard. Imperial soldiers flanked him on both sides and held laser rifles trained on me. When I reached the bottom of the ramp and stood in front of the admiral, he smiled at me, his eyes cold and glittering. Then he slapped me across the face so hard I stumbled to the floor.

My hands stung as I tried to catch my breath and grasp what he'd just done. My cheekbone ached, and tears stung the backs of my eyes. I'd never been struck before, and certainly not by a man.

"Get her up," he hissed.

Strong hands pulled me to my feet, but since the Zagrath soldiers wore black helmets, I couldn't see their faces. I held a hand to my throbbing cheek and bit my bottom lip to keep from crying. I would not give him the satisfaction of my tears.

"That was for stealing an imperial ship." His eyes became slits of fury as he backhanded me again, this time on my other cheek.

I didn't fall since I was being held up, but pain shot through my cheek, and I tasted blood. I closed my eyes and stifled a sob.

Kurmog leaned in, his foul breath hot. "That was for humiliating me. No bride of mine runs away."

I pulled away. "I'm not your bride."

"That is not for you to say. Your parents agreed to the match. You belong to the empire, and to me."

I straightened my shoulders. "I belong to Raas Toraan of the Vandar."

The admiral's gaze slid down my body, taking in the gown I wore. "So, I was right. The Vandar had you." His upper lip curled. "In more ways than one."

"I am his mate," I said, even though it hurt to talk.

Kurmog laughed, but the sound made me shiver. "You think I would honor anything those brutes do? You are not a bride of the Vandar. You are a whore, and you will be treated as one." He flicked a hand at me as he spun on his heel. "As soon as I destroy the Vandar colonies you led me to, I will show you how a whore is punished."

CHAPTER 38

Toraan

"Anything on long-range sensors?" I asked as I paced across the command deck.

Rolan did not look up from his standing console. "Not yet, Raas."

I growled. We'd left Zendaren as soon as we'd learned that the Zagrath ship was missing, but had yet to catch up to her. How long had she been gone before we'd given chase?

"Keep scanning," I ordered. "And let me know the moment you pick up anything."

There were murmurs of acknowledgment, but many of my command deck were still nursing hangovers from the banquet. Those who were not still drunk, that was.

We'd staggered to the horde and taken off quickly, but I knew I'd cut the planned visit much shorter than expected. Some of my raiders had barely seen their families before the call had gone out that we were leaving again on an emergency rescue mission.

I'll make it up to them, I told myself. As soon as we find Rachael, I'll take the horde back to Zendaren for an extended visit. *Tvek*, after we tracked down Rachael, I would need a long break myself.

I peered out the front of the ship again. As expected, there was little but the black vastness of space as we flew at our warbird's top speed toward the sector we'd left. I hoped my guess was correct. Where else would Rachael go, but someplace she knew? Even if it was someplace dangerous for her.

My stomach churned as I thought about her alone in the imperial shuttle. Not only did she have little experience flying, she was a sitting duck for any aliens looking for easy prey. Or worse, the imperial forces still searching for a runaway bride.

I spun on my heel and continued pacing, the movement the only thing keeping me from screaming. Part of me couldn't believe the female had actually run, and another wasn't a bit shocked. After all, she'd been running from a male when we'd taken her.

It stung that she'd felt she needed to run from me, as well. Then I thought of Lila's look of satisfaction when she'd told me about their conversation. I had no doubt that the Vandar female had been completely convincing. How had I ever cared about such a treacherous creature? My feelings for her seemed so childish to me now. What I felt for Rachael was different. It was real.

"Which is why I have to find her," I said, the leather of my battle kilt flapping against my thighs as I turned sharply.

"Raas?" Viken approached me, his eyes lowered. "We are approaching an imperial fleet."

I stared at him. "Out here? The Zagrath do not come this far away from their territory."

He inclined his head with a frown. "They do if they are tracking something. Powering up the Zagrath transport would have activated any beacons on it."

I closed my eyes briefly, absorbing the truth of his words. "She led them to us."

"Without intention, yes."

"What is their trajectory?" I asked, my heart pounding as I waited for his answer.

"They appear to be on a path to Zendaren."

I balled my hands into fists. This was all my fault. I'd brought the female on board, concocted a plan to strike back at the empire using her, and then lost her *and* brought the empire to my people's secret colonies.

"We need to protect the colonies," I said. "Order three quarters of the horde to turn back for Zendaren and shore up the planetary defenses. The rest of us will take on the imperial fleet here."

He gave a single nod and strode off to execute my orders. I didn't know if one quarter of the horde was enough against a large imperial fleet, but the Vandar people on Zendaren must be protected.

I peered out the front of the command deck as the hulking, gunmetal-gray ships came into view, my fingers tingling in anticipation of the battle which could very well be my last.

"Should we open fire, Raas?" Rolan asked. "Our invisibility shielding is giving us the upper hand."

As much as I wished to blow our enemy out of the sky, I could not be rash and impulsive. Not when my mate could be on board one of the ships.

"Hail them," I said.

Every raider froze, their gaze cutting to me. Vandar did not hail the enemy before we attacked. We did not practice diplomacy against an empire that had enslaved our people and destroyed our home world.

"Hail them, Raas?" Rolan's brow furrowed in obvious confusion.

I forgave him the momentary insubordination, but I leveled my gaze at him, nonetheless. "Those are my orders, *majak*. I want to know which of the ships has my mate. Hail Admiral Kurmog. I know he is behind this."

"Yes, Raas." Rolan tapped his fingers on his console, then looked up, his face solemn. "I have him. Onscreen?"

I pivoted to face the front as Viken took long steps to stand by my side. The imperial fleet vanished from view, replaced by an aged Zagrath officer. Even though his face was lined and his eyes heavily lidded, the admiral radiated power—and cruelty.

"I am Admiral Kurmog of the Zagrath Empire." He was unable to hide the sneer as he appraised me and my crew. "Who are you?"

"I am Raas Toraan of the Vandar." I curled my hand around the hilt of my battle axe. "I believe you have something of mine."

His cold eyes flared with what looked almost like glee as he reached a hand out of the frame and jerked something toward him. Rachael stumbled against him, but he held her arm in his grip, forcing her to look at me. Her face was bruised and puffy, and blood trickled from a cut in her bottom lip.

Viken stiffened next to me, and a low rumble passed through the raiders on deck. As merciless as we could be when we battled our enemy, no Vandar would ever strike a female.

"Is this the property you lost?" The admiral smiled, enjoyment dripping from his voice. "Is this the whore you stole from me?"

I tightened my grip on my axe, wanting nothing more than to slash off the head of the male who dared harm my mate. It no longer mattered to me that she did not share my love or my mating marks. She was mine, and no imperial admiral would take her from me. Or touch her again.

"She was never yours, Kurmog."

He laughed, glancing down at Rachael with a look of pure disgust. "Maybe not, but now that she's been sullied by a Vandar, she's good for nothing more than to be passed around my crew."

My gaze dropped to Rachael. She locked eyes with me as a single tear slid down her cheek and dripped off her chin onto the black swirl peeking out from under the neckline of her gown.

I sucked in a quick breath. Black marks were appearing on her skin. Mating marks. My mating marks.

CHAPTER 39

Toraan

"Raas." Viken's voice was so quiet I could barely hear him, but I knew from the urgent tenor of it that he'd seen what I'd seen. He hadn't turned toward me or even shifted his stance, but I felt the change in his energy.

I kept my gaze locked on the admiral, not wishing to betray what was happening to Rachael. "If you will not return the female, we have nothing more to say." I glanced at her briefly, my heart pounding at the sight of the marks appearing on her brown skin. "It is done."

I flicked my wrist to tell Rolan to take the admiral off-screen, letting out a breath when the Zagrath and Rachael vanished. As soon as the view of the chunky, gray battleships reappeared, Viken swiveled to face me.

"She has your marks, Raas."

I nodded, unable to speak. I'd never imagined I would see any female with my marks blooming on her skin, much less a human. I'd been convinced it wouldn't happen—couldn't happen—because she didn't feel for me as I felt for her. I'd been wrong.

Fear gripped me, and my stomach clenched. Now my mate—the female who shared my mating marks and my one true love—was being held by the enemy. Correction, she was being tortured by the enemy.

"We have to get her back," I said.

Rolan squared his shoulders. "She is Vandar now."

"And no one treats a Vandar mate like that," Viken growled. "I will tear his head off myself."

"You will leave the admiral to me." I coiled my fingers around the hilt of my axe, the desire to strike down the repulsive Zagrath making my fingers burn. I would have my revenge on him for striking my mate. And if he did what he said and passed her among his crew...? A rumble brewed in my throat, and I envisioned my feet thick in imperial blood. I would sever the limbs off every male who so much as looked at her.

"What are your orders, Raas?" Rolan asked. "We only have a quarter of the horde with us now."

I narrowed my eyes at the fleet that waited for us to strike. Our invisibility shielding hid us perfectly, until we opened fire. As soon as we targeted the imperial ships, we would be targets ourselves—with many fewer ships to lose.

"We cannot outshoot them." I scraped a hand through my hair. "So, we must outfly them."

Viken grinned. "Amoeba?"

Our Vandar attack pattern focused our offense in directed bursts, before shifting quickly to another target. It kept our enemy off-balance and unable to predict our next moves, plus, it made us more difficult to target.

"We need to weaken the ships protecting the lead battleship before I can sneak onto it," I said.

Rolan tapped his console as he transmitted encrypted instructions to the rest of the horde. "You'll be taking a raiding party onto the lead ship?"

"No party. Just me."

My *majak* and battle chief exchanged a glance, then looked at me.

"You cannot go onto a Zagrath ship by yourself, Raas," Viken said. "We are Vandar. We go together."

My throat tightened. I knew any of my raiders would walk gladly into death with me, but I could not ask it of them. I had been the one to get us in our current mess. I was the one who'd put our colonies at risk. I needed to be the one to make the sacrifice.

"You believe I will fail?" I cocked an eyebrow at Viken.

He bristled visibly. "I think the Zagrath expect you to come for her. It is a trap, Raas."

Of course, he was right. I was being lured onto the lead ship. There was no doubt in my mind that Admiral Kurmog wished to punish not only the female who humiliated him, but the Vandar Raas who claimed her before he could. I also knew I had no choice but to save her.

"It is done," I said. "You have your orders. Now, let's show these Zagrath what a fraction of a Vandar horde can do to them."

Rolan hesitated, but turned back to his console. Viken let out a grunt of disapproval but strode off to his own station.

"Black alert," one of the raiders called out before the command deck darkened, and purple, ambient lights glowed from the floor. "Brace for evasive maneuvers."

I joined Rolan at his post, setting my feet wide and holding the edge of the console as our ship dipped and banked hard right. We let loose a volley of laser fire at an imperial ship before peeling away and flying underneath it. I glanced down at Rolan's console, tracking the movements of our horde ships as we shifted like an undulating swarm around the neat rows of the Zagrath fleet. Though our ships weren't visible to the naked eye or possible to detect by our enemy, we were able to track them and ensure that we didn't crash into each other.

Red burst across our bow, and the ship shuddered. We were taking fire, but the hits weren't direct. Even though they could pinpoint where we'd fired from, we didn't stay in one place long enough to suffer direct impact.

"Our laser fire isn't doing much damage, Raas," Viken yelled, over the sounds of the battle. "Shall we unleash photon torpedoes?"

It was more difficult to fire a torpedo and move the ship out of the way, but it might be the only way to take out some of the smaller ships still acting as a buffer between us and the lead battleship. It was a risk, but we had little choice. "Affirmative. Fire at will."

Viken fired a pair of torpedoes, but only moments after they blew the side out of a Zagrath ship, our ship lurched violently to one side. Rolan and I were both knocked to our knees as sirens wailed.

"Report!" I pulled myself to my feet and saw that everyone else on the command deck was also righting themselves.

"Hull damage to our starboard," Viken said, before unleashing a torrent of Vandar curses. "They took out our other torpedo bays."

I breathed in the scent of smoke, and tried not to think what that meant. "The rest of the horde?"

"Damage reported on several ships, but none destroyed," Rolan said.

That was good news, but as I peered out to the battle on our view screen, I saw that the imperial fleet remained relatively undamaged. We didn't have the ships to take them out without being blown out of the sky, ourselves.

Rolan elbowed me, not a typical action for him. "Incoming transmission, Raas."

"I have no desire to speak to the Zagrath." And I couldn't bear to see Rachael and know that I was no closer to reaching her.

"It isn't from an imperial ship. It's from a Vandar one."

Had my uncle mustered forces to aid us? I shook my head. That didn't make sense, not when he needed ships to defend Zendaren.

Rolan paused with his fingers hovering above his console. "Actually, two incoming transmissions from two different ships."

"Onscreen," I said, my heart pounding.

When the figures of Raas Kratos and Raas Kaalek filled my command deck's view screen, I blinked several times. I hadn't seen my brothers since I was a boy. Although they looked similar to my memories of them, they were no longer dark-haired, lanky youth. They were massive, Vandar males, with chests covered by straps and armor. Despite their change, the same feelings of awe and longing filled me.

I cleared my throat. "It is good to see you, brothers."

Kratos was the first to drop his gruff stance, grinning widely. "Is that really you, Toraan? You are no longer a child."

"He's a Raas," Kaalek said, rolling his eyes, but also smiling. "Or do you forget that your younger brothers are also leaders of the Vandar, Kratos?"

This was the notorious Raas Kaalek? He was known for being ruthless and bloodthirsty, but here he was, teasing his older brother. And Kratos reminded me nothing of our cold and brutal father, who had been his mentor.

"There will be time for a family reunion later," Kratos said, "Right now, we're here to help you defeat the Zagrath and protect the colonies."

"How did you know?" I asked.

"We picked up chatter from the enemy. They've tried to keep their hunt for our colonies secret, but there are no secrets in such a vast empire," Kaalek said.

Kratos nodded. "Our hordes were en route to defend the colonies when we got a message from our uncle."

"But there is no communication between the colonies and hordes," I said.

Kratos shrugged. "He felt it was worth the risk."

"And we know about your mate." Kaalek's grin returned. "We both know about human mates and how impossible they can be."

"We thought you'd need all the help you could get," Kratos added.

Relief washed over me. "Our horde welcomes yours to the battle." I swallowed hard. "My mate is on the lead Zagrath ship, but I can't get onto it until we clear the blockade of ships guarding it."

"It is done," both Kratos and Kaalek said, raising fists into the air. "For Vandar!"

Every raider on my command deck bellowed the war cry, pounding their boots on the floor before the transmission ended and my brothers disappeared from the screen. I didn't wait for the floor to stop trembling before I turned and ran for the hangar bay.

It was time to rescue my mate.

CHAPTER 40

Rachael

Admiral Kurmog shoved me to the side the moment the transmission with the Vandar was cut off, and I caught myself on the corner of a white console before I hit the floor. A droplet of blood dripped onto my hand and another onto my chest. I wiped away the blood on my hand, then my gaze fell to the stain darkening the gold fabric of my gown. The blood on the gossamer bodice was almost as dark as the black marks curling across my skin.

I gasped and pressed a finger to my flesh, which was hot to the touch. I had mating marks. Toraan's mating marks.

"Take her to my ready room," the admiral barked, flicking a bony had at me. "I'll deal with her later."

I held my hands to my face and tried to cover my chest with my arms as two Zagrath soldiers grabbed me by the elbows and propelled me across the bridge. I didn't want Kurmog to see the marks. He was already furious, and my face was proof of that. I didn't want to experience him livid.

The admiral's ready room was attached to the bridge, so I was hurriedly pushed inside, and the door swished shut behind me. Unlike the rest of the bright and gleaming imperial battleship, the admiral's private space was more reminiscent of the Vandar warbird—dark and dimly-lit, with dusky furnishings and blue ambient light glowing in the recessed ceiling. But I knew very well that Kurmog was nothing like the Vandar.

Once I was alone, I tugged at the neckline of my dress to get a better look. The black swirling lines I'd seen so often on Toraan's chest were now on mine. I pressed my hand to the skin, startled by the burning sensation. The Raas had never mentioned that acquiring mating marks would be painful.

A pang of longing for Toraan made me stifle a sob. Seeing him on the screen had been torturous. He'd looked as imposing and menacing as ever, but I'd seen the hurt in his eyes. I'd betrayed him, and I'd led the enemy to his people. The people who had been hiding from the Zagrath's wrath for generations. All destroyed by one stupid human.

It was almost a cruel joke that my mating marks had developed only now, when I'd been recaptured by the empire. What were the chances that I'd ever see Toraan again, or that I'd live through Kurmog's torture? The admiral wasn't done with me—he'd made that perfectly clear—and as soon as he saw the marks on my skin, he'd probably have me executed. If I was lucky, he wouldn't do it on screen while Toraan watched.

I gave a rough shake of my head. Now was not the time to fall apart. Maybe Toraan had seen the marks. Maybe he understood that I hadn't left because I didn't care about him.

I scratched at my stinging flesh as I walked to the far wall of glass that looked out onto space and sank down onto the divan fronting it. There was no trace of any other ships aside from the imperial ones lined in front of the admiral's battleship, but the Vandar were out there. Toraan was out there. I could *feel* him.

I scratched my chest harder, trying to alleviate the burn of my flesh. Or maybe the marks on my skin just made me think I could feel him. I could sure as hell feel *them*.

The inky sky erupted into a shower of red laser fire, making me jump. Beams were flying from what appeared to be nothingness, but what I knew was the Vandar horde. My heart swelled as imperial ships were hit, and yells rose from outside the ready room.

The Vandar were attacking, which meant that Toraan wasn't giving up. I couldn't tear my eyes away from the battle, even though it was surreal to watch the Zagrath ships being attacked by invisible ones. No wonder the Vandar were called wraiths—they truly were like deathly wisps that appeared from nothing.

When the firing stopped, I held my breath. I'd seen no large explosion from where the Vandar had been firing. Had the raider ships retreated, or were they just regrouping?

"He wouldn't leave me," I whispered, pressing my fingers to my marks.

Then a massive explosion sent me flying off the divan and onto the floor. The two ships in front of ours had blown up, the blast making the window rattle as bits of the hull spiraled past. I pulled myself up to standing, as I gaped at the massive amount of laser fire bombarding the imperial fleet from all directions.

The sky pulsed red as the horde fired relentlessly, and more imperial ships tore apart. The Zagrath attempted to return fire, but their weapons appeared to be flying blind and making little contact.

I pumped a fist in the air. "Yes!"

I might have been on one of the enemy ships that was being fired upon, but I couldn't help cheering for Toraan.

Another hard jolt sent me staggering into a wall, but it didn't come from an explosion. More shouts on the bridge were followed by more jolts to the hull.

"We're being boarded!" The panicked yell from the imperial bridge officer made hope flutter in my chest.

The Vandar were coming. Toraan was coming.

The Zagrath were in chaos now. Flashing red lights replaced the blue ambient ones, as orders were bellowed outside the admiral's ready room and sirens shrieked. I shrank back, flattening myself against the wall and hoping they would forget about me.

The doors swished open and Kurmog stormed inside, his gaze sweeping the space and locking on me. So much for being forgotten.

He strode over to me and grabbed my arm, jerking me hard. "It seems the Vandar are looking for you."

"I'm sure if you turn me over, they'll spare your ship," I said, regretting my words as soon as they'd left my mouth.

The admiral slid his cold gaze to me, a vicious smile making him look more beast than man. "I have no intention of giving the Vandar what they want. I'd rather die."

I pulled against him as he tried to tug me with him. "Then where are you taking me?"

His reptilian smile widened. "To the nearest airlock, my dear."

Screams punctuated the air outside the room as a heavy drumbeat of pounding feet thundered onto the bridge. Kurmog froze as the door slid open and three Vandar raiders rushed inside, battle axes dripping with blood.

My knees almost buckled when I realized that the raider in the middle was Toraan, although the two equally muscled and armored raiders beside him looked strikingly similar.

"This one's mine," Toraan growled, stepping forward, his eyes flashing with fury.

Kurmog tightened his grip on my arm. "She will never be yours."

Toraan's gaze went to my marks for the briefest of moments. "It is done."

As the admiral reached for his blaster, I wrenched my arm from his grip and dove for the floor, my hands bracing my fall at the same moment Toraan's axe blade severed Kurmog's head. The admiral's body remained upright for a few more seconds, even as his head rolled across the floor, coming to rest against the wall, the cold, dead eyes wide with shock.

Toraan lifted me up and crushed me to him, his strong arms keeping my shaky legs from buckling. "Are you unhurt?"

My hands slipped on the blood smeared across his chest, and I peered up at him. "I'm fine. Are you?"

"Only blood from the enemy." He held me away from him, his focus shifting to my chest.

"I got them," I managed to say, even as my voice quavered.

He traced one finger over the marks on my chest as he stared at them. Then he pulled his chest straps aside so I could see that his marks had expanded and now stretched over his shoulders and down his stomach. "I, as well."

"I guess this means you're stuck with me," I said, trying to smile, even though my lips trembled.

Toraan lifted my hand to his lips and kissed my open palm. "My Raisa."

Before I could burst into tears, one of the raiders who had flanked Toraan cleared his throat.

"Might I suggest you continue this once we get the *tvek* off this ship and have blown it up?"

Toraan glanced back at both Vandar, who were waving for us to join them in backing from the room. He pulled me close to him as we all rushed from the room, a blast shaking the ship.

"Who are they?" I asked as we ran behind the pair of enormous raiders. They wore shoulder armor like Toraan and radiated command.

"My older brothers," he bellowed over the thundering explosions rocking the ship.

One of the Vandar glanced at me over his shoulder, never slowing his pace. "Welcome to the family! I'd say it isn't usually like this, but I'd be lying."

"And a Raas never lies," the other brother added with a half grin. "Brace yourself for a rocky ride, human."

CHAPTER 41

Toraan

"I didn't think I would live to see this," my uncle said, his back to the stone balustrade as we gathered on the balcony overlooking the feasting hall. "Your father would have been pleased."

Kratos flinched next to me, but Kaalek was the one who spoke. "You were the one who brought us back together, Raas. We have you to thank for the reunion of the hordes."

"It is we who owe a debt of gratitude to you," Raas Maassen, said as we stood across from him, the preparations for the celebration banquet bustling beneath us. "You destroyed the imperial fleet and saved the colonies from being discovered."

I looked at my feet. He was right that the three hordes had come together and blown the Zagrath fleet from the sky—as soon as we'd escaped from the lead battleship and gotten Rachael out of danger—but the fact remained that it had been my decision that had led the empire to Zendaren in the first place. "I am grateful to my brothers. Without them—"

"It was our honor to join you in battle," Kratos said, cutting off my confession that without them the Vandar would not have prevailed and our people would have been decimated.

"Agreed," Kaalek said. "There is little I have enjoyed more than watching my younger brother slay a Zagrath admiral. Well, aside from the things my mate does to me. Those I enjoy more."

Kratos shot him a look, but the old Raas only laughed.

"You have changed little since you were boys."

My memories of Kratos and Kaalek were so faint that I'd always assumed I'd imagined them, but the teasing felt familiar. As did the quick tempers and fights that flared up faster than brush fire. Kaalek and Kratos had almost come to blows multiple times as we'd raced through the imperial battleship searching for Rachael and striking down imperial soldiers. I'd been grateful we'd found her before the two had taken to wrestling each other on the floor.

"Zendaren is much as I remember it," Kratos said, peering around. "Even though I have been away for longer than I can remember, it still feels like home."

"It will always be your home," the old Raas said.

Kratos rocked back on his heels. "Is there room for another Raas who wishes to hang up his battle axe?"

Kaalek and I both swung our gazes to him.

"You?" Kaalek gaped at him.

Kratos cleared his throat and his cheeks flushed. "Astrid is with child. Although she insists she can continue to serve with me on our warbird and as Raisa to the horde, I do not want to take the risk."

Kaalek's mouth fell open even farther. "Tara's sister is pregnant?"

The red on Kratos' face deepened.

"The first human-Vandar child," our uncle said softy, shaking his head. "Another thing I never thought I'd see—or imagined possible."

From the look on Kaalek's face, he was thinking the same thing I was. It appeared Vandar males *could* impregnate human females. We could both become fathers, as well.

"Congratulations, brother." I clapped him on the back. "You are sure you wish to give up your horde?"

Kratos gave a single nod. "My *majak*, Bron, will take over as Raas. There is no one I trust more to be a just and victorious Raas."

Kaalek snapped out of his shock. "I wish you all the best. Tara is happy flying with the horde for now, but you can be sure we will return once the baby is born. I have never been an uncle before." He nudged his elder brother. "Someone will need to show your child how to have fun."

Kratos grinned and shook his head. "Lokken preserve me." He twisted his head to look at me. "And what of you, Tor? I saw that you and your mate resolved whatever differences parted you."

"That was hard to miss on the ride off the imperial battleship," Kaalek muttered. "I should know. I was standing next to the two of them."

Kratos and Kaalek both laughed, and even though I tried to keep my expression stony, I finally joined their laughter.

"Rachael wishes to fly with me. She claims she hasn't seen enough of the galaxy, yet."

"I hope she likes pleasure planets, if she's taking her tour of the galaxy on a horde ship," Kaalek said.

"Actually," I grinned at my brothers. "She got quite a few tips from a madam the last time we docked with a pleasure ship. I would not mind seeing what she picked up on a pleasure planet."

Kaalek's eyebrows shot up. "And here I was thinking your mate was as sweet and innocent as she looks."

"As someone who took a mate who *was* innocent, I promise you that humans are full of surprises," Kratos said, patting me on the shoulder. "Trust me. You have only scratched the surface, brother."

Kaalek bobbed his head up and down. "I'll second that, and I have the scratches to prove it."

"What are you bragging about now, you arrogant ass?" Kaalek's mate Tara pushed the balcony drape aside as she, Astrid, and Rachael joined us.

All three females were dressed in long gowns for the banquet, with their hair artfully arranged. Although all of our mates were striking, I only had eyes for Rachael.

Astrid giggled as she sidled up to Kratos and watched me staring at my mate. "Didn't we do a good job?"

I nodded mutely. Rachael wore a strapless, red dress that poured over her curves. The bruises on her face had faded and been skillfully covered. The only marks on her skin were the black ones curling across her cleavage and up to the hollow of her throat.

She wrapped a hand around my waist, her gaze going to my matching marks. "I missed you."

"I think the rest of us should go downstairs," my uncle said, striding forward and patting Astrid on the hand. "I want to hear more about when I'm becoming a great-uncle."

The blonde flushed as the two couples and the old Raas moved off the balcony, and the curtain fell behind them.

"She's really excited about the baby," Rachael said. "It will be the first human and Vandar child ever."

"I am happy for her and Kratos."

She put a hand on my chest. "It made me think of something. You know the Raisa suite attached to your quarters?"

I tilted my head at her as I waited for her to continue. "Yes?"

"It would be perfect for a nursery." She fluttered a hand in the air. "Once it's cleared of its sad mojo."

"Nursery?" This was not a Vandar word or one that translated.

Splotches of pink mottled the brown of her cheeks. "A room for a baby."

Now my face warmed. "I like that idea."

She grinned up at me. "And I like your brothers and their mates. It's nice to talk to other humans who are mated to Vandar."

"What did you learn?"

She mimed locking her lips. "Vandar aren't the only ones good at secrets."

"Is this more about babies?" I pulled her closer to me. "I have ways of making you talk, you know."

She gave me a wicked smile. "Not up here on a balcony, you don't."

I spun her around so she was facing the stone railing, and bent her over. "Never dare a Vandar."

She braced her hands on the stone and looked back at me over her shoulder. Her eyes were wide, but a smile teased the corner of her mouth. "But there are all those people below us, and anyone could walk through those curtains."

I lifted her dress, moaning when I saw that she wore nothing underneath. Her round ass was bare, and as I tipped it up and spread her legs, I could see that she was already wet for me. "Then maybe you should reconsider keeping secrets from your Raas."

She bit her bottom lip and twitched her ass at me. "Never."

I reached under my battle kilt and fisted my cock before dragging it through her folds. "Then it is done." I thrust myself deep inside her, as she arched her back and gasped.

"Toraan," she gritted out.

I bent forward, holding myself deep and putting one hand over her mouth. "Shhh, mate. If you make a sound, everyone will know I'm fucking you. All they'll have to do is look up, and they'll see that my cock is buried in your tight, little cunt."

She made a small, keening noise that was muffled by my hand.

I dragged my cock out and then drove it deep again. "Do you want to scream? Do you want them to know that you're being fucked by your Raas?"

She nodded, writhing against me. I tugged the top of her dress down so that her breasts popped out, then I used my free hand to caress her firm nipples, making her moan even louder into my hand.

I leaned closer to her ear as I hammered into her, flesh slapping against flesh. "No screaming, mate, or they'll see your perfect breasts bouncing as I fuck you."

With a gasp, she bit down hard on my finger as her body rippled around my cock. The pain from her bite mingled with the sensations storming through my body, and I thrust myself deep as I exploded. I threw my head back, but swallowed the roar, holding my cock inside her as my release blinded me. I finally sank down, curling my body over hers, and dropping my hand from her mouth.

Rachael was panting, and she tugged her dress up as she twisted her head around to meet my eyes. "This doesn't mean I'm telling you."

My cock was still inside her, but I slid my tail up the inside of her thigh until I found her slick bundle of nerves. "Who said I was done with my interrogation?"

EPILOGUE

General Hardin slammed his hand onto the desk, and his tablet rattled against the chrome surface. "How the fuck did this happen?"

The imperial soldier facing him flinched but kept his shoulders stiff, as if bracing for more of an onslaught. "Unclear, General. The last communication we received from Admiral Kurmog indicated that he'd located the Vandar colonies, but no coordinates were ever sent."

"And the fleet he was commanding?"

"Destroyed." The soldier stared straight ahead as he delivered the news.

"The entire fleet?" The general shook his head. "Impossible. He was leading over twenty ships, including his own Mercury-class battleship."

"We sent ships to search for them, but there was nothing but debris from a battle. Significant debris."

General Hardin rubbed a hand over his forehead, then dragged it across his close-cropped hair. "If the admiral and his fleet had survived, he would have made contact." He braced his hands on the desktop. "Was it the Vandar?"

"By all accounts, sir."

The general grunted, then waved a hand in dismissal. "That will be all. Send in the operative waiting outside."

The soldier's face registered fear for a moment, before he spun on his heel and left the Zagrath general's office. The door had not slid shut again, before the operative stepped inside.

Hardin looked up and straightened, grasping his hands behind his back as he surveyed the imperial assassin. Although he'd never personally deployed the trained killer, he'd heard tales. Although he considered himself hardened to battle, the tales about empire's most notorious assassin had made even his blood run cold.

"You know what happened to our fleet?" he asked, well aware that Zagrath headquarters had been buzzing with little else.

"I do."

The general walked out from behind his desk. "I've called you in because I want someone who can infiltrate the Vandar."

"To kill them?"

"Not at first. They are like insects. No matter how many we kill, they keep coming. No, I want someone who can get information we can use to bring them down from the inside. Admiral Kurmog managed to discover the location of one of the Vandar secret colonies—or so he claimed—but he was defeated before he could pass along the information. I need someone who will not be distracted by a personal vendetta."

"I have no personal connection to the Vandar."

The general smiled. "Not yet, you don't."

"Sir?"

"Your mission is to be taken by the newest Vandar Raas. From what we know, he is unmated. Seduce him, win his trust, and discover what we need to know to bring down the Vandar." General Hardin shrugged one shoulder. "Then you can kill him."

The raven-haired beauty inclined her head and gave him a smile that had lured many a male into her trap and to their death. "Consider it done."

Thank you for reading PILLAGED! If you liked this alien barbarian romance, you'll love PURSUED, book 4 in the series.

My task is to infiltrate the Vandar raider horde and seduce Raas Bron--then kill him. As an assassin for the empire, it's a job I've done countless times. I should have no problem sharing a bed with the gorgeous warlord and then cutting his throat. If only I could ignore the way his touch ignites me—and threatens to destroy my mission.

One-click PURSUED Now>

Want a BONUS EPILOGUE featuring all three Vandar warlords and their human mates? Join my VIP Reader group and get PILLAGED AGAIN to see what happens after the welcome home banquet!

https://BookHip.com/DWLCX

This book has been edited and proofed, but typos are like little gremlins that like to sneak in when we're not looking. If you spot a typo, please report it to: tana@tanastone.com
Thank you!!

ALSO BY TANA STONE

Raider Warlords of the Vandar Series:

POSSESSED

PLUNDERED

PILLAGED

PURSUED

Alien Academy Series:

ROGUE (also available in AUDIO)

The Tribute Brides of the Drexian Warriors Series:

TAMED (also available in AUDIO)

SEIZED (also available in AUDIO)

EXPOSED (also available in AUDIO)

RANSOMED (also available in AUDIO)

FORBIDDEN (also available in AUDIO)

BOUND (also available in AUDIO)

JINGLED (A Holiday Novella)

CRAVED (also available in AUDIO)

STOLEN

SCARRED

The Barbarians of the Sand Planet Series:

BOUNTY (also available in AUDIO)

CAPTIVE (also available in AUDIO)

TORMENT (also available on AUDIO)

TRIBUTE

SAVAGE

CLAIM

TANA STONE books available as audiobooks!

Alien Academy Series:

ROGUE on AUDIBLE

BARBARIANS OF THE SAND PLANET

BOUNTY on AUDIBLE

CAPTIVE on AUDIBLE

TORMENT on AUDIBLE

TRIBUTE BRIDES OF THE DREXIAN WARRIORS

TAMED on AUDIBLE

SEIZED on AUDIBLE

EXPOSED on AUDIBLE

RANSOMED on AUDIBLE

FORBIDDEN on AUDIBLE

BOUND on AUDIBLE

CRAVED on AUDIBLE

AUTHOR'S NOTE

I hope you enjoyed PILLAGED! If you did, please consider leaving a quick review on Amazon. It can even be as short as one sentence. Reviews help readers like you find new books and new-to-them authors. They also make my day! :-)

Click here to leave a quick review!

Thank you so much! Wonderful readers like you are why I love writing!
xoxo,
Tana

ABOUT THE AUTHOR

Tana Stone is a bestselling sci-fi romance author who loves sexy aliens and independent heroines. Her favorite superhero is Thor (with Aquaman a close second because, well, Jason Momoa), her favorite dessert is key lime pie (okay, fine, *all* pie), and she loves Star Wars and Star Trek equally. She still laments the loss of *Firefly*.

She has one husband, two teenagers, and two neurotic cats. She sometimes wishes she could teleport to a holographic space station like the one in her tribute brides series (or maybe vacation at the oasis with the sand planet barbarians). :-)

She loves hearing from readers! Email her any questions or comments at tana@tanastone.com.

Want to hang out with Tana in her private Facebook group? Join on all the fun at: https://www.facebook.com/groups/tanastonetributes/

Copyright © 2020 by Broadmoor Books

Cover Design by Croci Designs

Editing by Tanya Saari

All rights reserved.

No part of this book may be reproduced in any form or by any electronic or mechanical means, including information storage and retrieval systems, without written permission from the author, except for the use of brief quotations in a book review.

This is a work of fiction. Names, characters, places, and incidents are the products of the author's imagination or are used fictitiously and are not to be construed as real. Any resemblance to actual events, locales, organizations, or persons, living or dead, is entirely coincidental.

Printed in Great Britain
by Amazon